"Love Stories?"

By

Terry Finley

ISBN: 978-0-6151-8725-9
PUBLISHED BY KERAMEUS PUBLISHING

Printed in the United States of America

Dedication

This collection of short stories is dedicated to my mother Aline Tubbs and to my brother David Lee Finley.

If you would not be forgotten,
as soon as you are dead and rotten,
either write things worth reading,
or do things worth the writing.

- Benjamin Franklin

I have been successful probably because I have always realized that I knew nothing about writing and have merely tried to tell an interesting story entertainingly.

- Edgar Rice Burroughs

Unless a writer is extremely old when he dies, in which case he has probably become a neglected institution, his death must always be seen as untimely. This is because a real writer is always shifting and changing and searching. The world has many labels for him, of which the most treacherous is the label of Success.

- James Baldwin

Table of Contents

An Angel in Disguise

Fountainville was a sprawling city of 25,000 located between the Blue Valley Desert and the Pearl Sea, but everybody referred to it as the hellhole because it was always so hot. Most of its citizens worked in the tourist industry. One could read about the city in the major encyclopedias because of its elaborate fountains.

Outside the city at the edge of the desert lived a tribe of native herdsmen. These people had thick, wavy hair, red to reddish brown. Their eyes were generally hazel green. Their height ranged from five feet to seven feet; their bodies tended to be gangly. Their skin was light creamy brown, and their faces were angular. There were few words spoken between the city people and the natives.

Wiley Jenugah was a thirty-eight year old man, big-boned, light brown skin, with a thin, hollow-cheeked face. He had fine, strawberry blond hair and blue-grey eyes. He worked at the docks and was aggressive but flighty. Julia Buhaior was twenty-four, slight, with ebony skin and a thin, high-cheekboned face. She wore fine straight brown hair and had green eyes. She worked as an astrologer, brave by nature, but crabby. Wiley and Julia were brother and sister.

"I wish the moon would never go away and the sun would never rise," Julia said.

Wiley's right foot splashed in the waves and his left hand rested under his head. "If it were not for showing up at the dock and getting paid, I'd agree with you."

"Tell me again about our parents. How old was I?" Julia asked.

"You were three. They went on an all-day fishing excursion, and the boat never came back into the harbor. The herdsmen even helped the city people look for the boat. It was never found, and there were no survivors. It's that simple."

"What do you mean: it's that simple? It's never that simple. I never knew my parents. I grew up with a big brother."

"That's not all bad."

"I wanted my parents; I want them now."

"Julia, isn't it about time you grew up? That's not going to happen."

"Never. Not until I have a mother and a father."

"Well, what you have is a big brother who did the best he could."

"I know that. I know that." Julia kissed Wiley on the forehead.

The sun began inching up over the horizon, and the moon disappeared in a matter of ten minutes. Wiley left the beach to get ready to return to the docks. Julia turned on her side with her back to the sun. She took out the latest paper on the zodiac. It was funny to her how she could memorize every issue within two days of it coming in the mail. Silently, she cursed the sun and longed for the moon. In that issue there was an article about the Egyptians and the Mesopotamians. She liked studying the history of astrology. In fact she had a fair sized library in her room.

Samantha, a friend of Julia's, came walking along the beach. The sea water dripped off her onto the sand making tiny puddles. "Good morning. What are you reading?"

"Astrology."

"I figured that. What's it about?'

"This edition is more of the history. It's about the Egyptians and the Mesopotamians. Do you know about them?"

"No, not at all. Let's go feed the goats."

"Why not? The sun's already ruined the day."

"Julia, I love the sun. Perhaps Capricorn will be with the other goats."

Julia sat up. "He just might be. That would make my day. I love that goat. I just wish he were not so wild. It's hard to even pat him."

Samantha toweled off and took her clothes out of her basket. Julia stood up and collected her things. They walked into Fountainville. Julia stopped along the way and got six new carrots and some grain. They walked through the city pass several fountains, most active, a few dry and decrepit. They walked side by side, and Samantha did most of the talking. A short distance out from the city on the desert side rolling hills separated the city from the desert. There the goats spent most of the day.

Rocks and stones littered the path up to and through the hills. Usually one could hear the natives in the distance. That day there was no wind, and the silence was peaceful and full of calm. The path took them higher into the hills. At last they could hear the goats even before they saw them. Samantha stopped and enjoyed the moment. Julia pulled her on in the direction of the goats.

Julia slipped on a rock and caught herself before she fell to the ground. Samantha looked out toward the goats and just stared.

"What do you see?" Julia asked.

"I'm not sure. For a minute I thought it was you."

"Me? What are you talking about?"

"Be quiet and let's go see."

Julia didn't like being bossed about, but her curiosity had the better of her. "Okay. Lead on."

The two women were not crooks, and they were not spies. However, they looked deep in themselves to find the tricks needed to sneak upon the other female. She was alone as is the custom with the natives caring for the goats. She looked to be in her early twenties. Her skin was sooty, almost black. She had a thin face, and her cheekbones were prominent. Her hair was rustic in color, long and straight. She cared for the goats with the prestige of authority. She watched the goats with care and didn't realize the presence of Julia and Samantha.

"Look!" Samantha whispered. "It's you. There's two of you."

"Shhh, be quiet. This is weird. There's an explanation. I don't ever remember reading about something like this in my books and papers."

"If that's not you, it's your twin."

"I admit she sure does look like me, and she likes goats, too."

Samantha slipped on a rock and twisted her right ankle. She cried out in pain. Julia gave her a disgusted look and said, "Shut up, or she'll hear us."

Too late. The native woman not only heard but took off like a scared rabbit. In a matter of seconds she was out of sight. Julia and

Samantha stood there and looked at each other, Samantha massaging her angle.

"I wonder how Wiley would explain this?" Samantha asked.

"I wonder too. I've always wished he'd be completely open with me. I get the feeling he's holding something back. She did look like me, but I've seen people who look alike before. It's a freak of nature."

"There!" Samantha exclaimed, pointing to the next hill.

"What?"

"Capricorn."

"Great. Let's go feed him." Julia almost totally forgot about the native woman.

They eased over to the top of the next hill, Samantha hobbling and panting as they went along. Capricorn raised his head but did not run away. He was a big goat, white haired with a long goatee. He watched as they approached. It was as if he had been raised by humans and later let loose in the desert area.

Samantha sat down on a boulder and rubbed her ankle. It was swelling and turning black and blue already. Julia tiptoed up to the goat and patted its head. The goat smelt the few carrots and grain and sniffed her pockets. Julia fed Capricorn and talked to him like they were old friends.

Across the city on the waterfront at the docks Wiley helped a co-worker take a wagon off a ship from Spain. They were telling jokes and sweating in the sun. They had been close friends for years. Somehow they started talking about their families.

"You know, Wiley, my sister wants to have a baby. Her husband is doing okay."

"Well," Wiley replied. "I just wish Julia would get married."

"Is she still as cranky as ever?"

"Worse than ever. She's always asking about our parents."

"Have you ever told her the truth?"

"No, of course not. I don't want to hurt her."

"Is she still into astrology?"

"More than ever. Her room is covered with those books, and now she's even getting new stuff daily in the mail."

"Does she really believe that or is she just kidding?"

"I think she's really serious. She's found this wild goat she's named Capricorn."

"You're kidding."

"Nope. I bet she went to feed him today. She claims it'll bring her and me really good fortune and happiness in the future."

"How can a goat bring you fortune and happiness, unless you kill it and eat it?"

"That's what I think, but Julia's gotten attached to it."

Later Julia brought lunch to the docks for Wiley. The basket contained fresh milk, bread, bacon and sausage and two apples. She also brought fresh water. Samantha followed as she still nursed her ankle. There was a serious, angry, and pondering look on Julia's face.

Michael, Wiley's co-worker friend, saw them coming first. "Uh oh! Here comes Julia. That look on her face does not look pleasant."

Julia dropped the food and drinks abruptly beside Wiley. "Here's your lunch. I have a question, and I want a straight, honest answer."

"What could be so serious?"

"Here's what: do I have a sister?"

Michael patted Wiley on the shoulder. "I'll leave now; I need to get my lunch." He bid them all adieu.

"Why are you always harping on this? Why don't you just leave it alone?"

"Wiley," Julia raised her voice. "Do I, or don't I? It's that simple."

"Alright sit down while I eat, and I'll tell you."

The sun was almost directly over head. Sea gulls screamed and raced about. The sea waves came in and went out. A tourist boy and girl walked on the beach, holding hands. One could smell sweat and dead fish. They walked over and sat down on the dock, their feet dangling slightly over the water. Wiley offered them some food; they both declined. Wiley was procrastinating, and Julia was anxiously awaiting his answer.

"Are you sure you want to know all this?"

"Yes, get on with it, Wiley."

Wiley drank some milk and took a small bite of bread. "Yes, you have a sister. In fact, she's a twin sister."

"Then why the big secret?"

"That was your mother's wish."

"My mother. What do you mean my mother?"

"That's it; she's your mother, not my mother. They adopted me when I was five. My parents died in some epidemic."

"You mean we're not….?"

"That's right. We're not even half brother and sister."

Samantha interrupted, "I told you that woman looked just like you."

"What woman?" Wiley asked.

Julia was not naïve. There would be no easy form of remedy to deflate her heaven sent self-esteem. She had the necklace, but should Wiley tell her about the hotel room? He waited for what seemed like hours for Julia to answer his question. Instead Samantha and Julia stood up and went through a whispering spell.

"What woman?" Wiley asked again, almost demanding.

Julia told Wiley all about the trip to the hills, every detail including Samantha's ankle and Capricorn. Then there was the part about the young woman. They had not spoken to her; she ran away when Samantha screamed. She looked so much like Julia. It was spooky. A sister, a twin sister, would explain it all.

Wiley decided to go ahead and tell the whole truth. Julia's mother was married to a man from England. They adopted Wiley when he was five years old and brought him back to Fountainville. The man owned a couple of ships and was in the transport business; he had done very well. However, he was killed aboard one of his ships when eleven pirates tried to hijack the ship and steal its cargo.

Julia's mother had almost gone insane with grief. She started drinking and running with different men and some of the city's low-life. One evening when she had walked outside the city toward the desert, she met one of the native men, about her age. Although it was taboo for both the natives and the city people, the two of them started an affair. Sexually, it consisted of a one-night stand in the local hotel. That union resulted in Julia's mother's pregnancy.

The native man took her as his wife and lived with her out with the natives. The natives were quicker to accept her than the city folk were to accept him. However, the pregnancy turned out to be twins. In the native culture twins were taboo. It was evil and unnatural for such to happen. It was the work of the devil. One child had to go. That meant death for one. Julia's mother could not do that. She picked Julia's twin sister to keep and sent Wiley and Julia back to the city to make it on their own.

Wiley was only sixteen years old. However, he managed to take care of Julia with the help of an old, old lady who lived on the edge of the city. She had been at one time friends with Julia's mother. She kept all this a secret up to her dying day. Wiley began working with the ships at the dock and had been there ever since. Julia's mother had never attempted to contact them. She was content to live her life out with the natives at the edge of the desert.

"You never saw her again?" Julia asked.

"No, never," Wiley replied.

"Is she still alive?"

"I don't have any idea."

"You mean she's lived so close to us all these years and never cared enough to see about us?"

"That's exactly what I mean?"

"That bitch. I hate her."

"You wouldn't leave it alone. You had to know. Do you feel better knowing the truth?"

"No, but I know the truth?"

"She could have left you to die."

"That bitch!"

"What will you do?" Samantha asked.

"Go find her, if she's still alive."

A large cloud blanketed out the sun's rays, and darkness fell on the docks. Wiley reached for more milk and bread and sausage. Samantha rubbed her ankle. Julia sat there and let her mind fume. It was obvious she was thinking and her anger level was rising. The big cloud moved on, and the sun beamed as before. Several dock hands were returning from lunch.

"Can I give you some advice?" Wiley asked.

"What?" Julia snapped.

"Forget it and leave it alone."

"Never; I want to see my mother face to face. What happened to my father?"

"I'm not sure; he might still be living with your mother."

"Wouldn't that be fun; we could all throw a party."

"A heartbreak party. You're just asking for trouble and to get hurt."

"We'll see. It's my life, and I want my say."

"When are you going? Where will you go?" Samantha asked.

"I think I'll go this evening. I'll just start following the paths through the hills until I get to the natives."

"Is that wise?"

"Who cares? Right now I'm mad and sad and I have to go."

Later Julia set out by herself to find her mother. Samantha had wanted to go, but Julia made up her mind to go alone. She wanted to confront her mother alone. However, she had no idea what she was going to say. The sun began slipping down beyond the horizon and shadows danced around the hills. Despite Julia's attitude and thoughts the scene was simply beautiful.

When Julia topped one of the hills, she saw Capricorn and other goats out in the distance. A search of her pockets revealed she had nothing to offer her favorite sign and goat. That was not a good omen she thought. She hoped things were not going to turn sour from the very start. If they were going to get sour, she wanted it to come from what she would say to her mother.

Beyond Capricorn and some other goats were two native boys watching the goats. Julia decided to ask them about the woman that looked like her. She knew that the boys were not supposed to talk to city people, but she was determined.

When the boys saw Julia, a sense of fright overcame them. They started to run.

"Wait!" Julia called out.

The two boys stopped in their tracks, pointed at Julia, and began whispering. Julia knew what they were discussing: two look-a-likes. In their culture that was taboo. It was scary how two peoples could live so close together and live such different life styles.

"Do you know the woman who looks like me?"

They shook their heads 'yes'.

"Where?"

They pointed back in the direction of their village.

"Will you show me?"

They shook their heads 'no'.

"Don't worry; it'll be okay."

They shook their heads 'no' again.

Julia began to chant and circle them. This action scared the two boys. They were frozen and could not run. Round and round went Julia, chanting. Finally, the two boys shook their heads 'yes'.

Julia pointed toward their village and followed them. They led her into the village like the head of a parade. The boys were afraid and amazed at the same time. The villagers stared and pointed and whispered. It was beginning to get dark. The women sat around fires of wood and straw; boiling pans hung over the fires. Some men sat in the middle of the village and observed all that went on.

The boys ran ahead and talked to one of the women. Presently the woman who was the sister of Julia came out of one hut. All the women gasped and looked shocked. One of them was supposed to be dead, but the elders of the village knew Julia was not dead. In fact, they had already punished Julia's mother.

"Why are you here?" the sister demanded. "You bring us nothing but trouble. Our lady is old and feeble. She does not need a visit from you."

"Well, I need to see her. I just learned the truth about you and me and our mother. I did not have any idea until I saw you in the hills."

"Neither did I. All this time I thought our lady had an accident after I was born. Now I learn the elders punished her for not allowing you to die. Our lady has suffered enough."

"What do you mean she suffered too much, and why do you call her 'our lady'?"

"Our father was the chief's son. He disappeared after our lady's accident. I was always told he died in the desert. Our lady was to be the queen of the village. No queen reigns in the condition of our lady."

"What is her condition?" Julia asked.

"Come, and I will show you."

The sister led Julia past two huts and stopped outside the third. "Don't say a word. Just look and see what our lady went through because of you."

"What is wrong with her?"

"The elders burned her eyes shut and cut out her tongue. She cannot see, and she cannot speak."

"They did this to her because of me?"

"Yes, it is bad to have two of one child. One must go."

"Let me see; I will keep quiet. I just want to see for myself. I always wanted to have my parents."

The sister drew back the curtain and led Julia into the one-room hut. The only light came from a small fire in one corner. There was an old lady with white hair sitting beside the wall holding a baby lamb. She was rocking it like a baby. Every once in awhile the lamb would lick the old lady's arm.

The lady had large black scars where her eyes were supposed to be. She rocked herself as she rocked the lamb. If Julia ever wondered what she would look like as an old lady, she now knew. The likeness between the old lady and Julia was remarkable.

Julia tried to feel hatred and contempt for the old lady. In her mind she tried and tried to say, "bitch; you're a bitch," but the words wouldn't form. All she was able to do was run from the hut out to the hills and cry. She found Capricorn, petted him for a long time and cried.

When she returned to the city, she found Wiley and Samantha waiting for her.

"Well?" they both asked.

"I have a mother. She's our lady, and she loves me."

My Water Falls

Niagara Falls. That was the spot, when I was a kid. My parents treated me well when they took me there twice on vacation. Then, later, when I was twenty-five I visited water falls all over the world. My parents were killed in an auto accident after I finished high school and before I joined the navy. They left me about ten thousand dollars. On my trip around the world (being egged on by my travels in the navy) I spent most of that money and all of the money I saved while in the navy.

To be blunt: I love water falls. That was to be my saving grace, and my down fall.

After my tour of the world, I returned to Alabama, my home state. I lived northwest of Birmingham. My sister and her family lived in Huntsville. I had nothing left of interest to keep me in Walker county. I decided to go visit my sister and then to work my way on a tour up to Canada and down to Mexico. What work, I had no idea.

I stayed three days with my sister; her kids almost drove me nuts.

"Uncle Keith, ride me piggy-back."

"I just rode you piggy-back for twenty minutes."

"Ride me piggy-back again, Uncle Keith."

"One more time, and then I have a bus or a train or something to catch."

I left Huntsville headed north. It took me several months to make much progress. I spent time in lots of kitchens washing dishes. I even bought the supplies and made me up a top notch shoe shine kit. I spent time on street corners buffing shoes. The tips came to more than my charges to shine shoes. I never went hungry or never lacked a place to sleep.

I went by Niagara Falls going to and coming back from Canada. That certainly has to be, hands down, the most beautiful place God ever made. I wish I could make an enormous rock platform jetting out from the falling water. I would live there the rest of my life. I would, however, need to invent some kind of good ear plugs to muffle the noise.

One afternoon as the sun set, I stood at the top looking down and blurted out loud, "I'm in love with this place."

A couple from Japan stood behind me taking picture after picture. "We do, too."

I got back on the bus and started working my way south again. I took a different route but with the same routine and same chores. In two months I knocked on my sister's door and again took my nephews for a piggy-back ride.

With a hearty "Hiyo, Silver, Away" I resumed my trek to Mexico. And I have to admit this is where my story turned nasty. I wish I had simply gotten lost in the wilds between Guntersville and Fort Payne.

In Corpus Christi, Texas I took a tour bus to Laredo and from there we traveled across the border to Monterrey, Mexico. In Laredo a lady who looked to be about thirty got on the bus and sat next to me. Her name was Lou Ann. She was from the southern part of New Jersey. She'd never heard of Walker County, Alabama, and I'd never heard of whatever the name of the city was in New Jersey. We didn't talk for the longest time. I looked out the window, and she read some articles from a journal on Hernando Cortez.

"This your first visit to Mexico?" I asked.

"No, I live in Saltillo," she replied.

"Do you enjoy living there?"

"From the very first day I moved there."

"What do you do?" I asked, pointing to her magazine.

"I have degrees in languages and archeology from Harvard University and the University of Chicago. Originally, I came to Mexico to study and do research. Hernando Cortez is a hobby of mine," she said, looking down at her journal.

"How are things now?"

"Not too good," she replied, implying she really did not care to discuss it further.

I sat next to the window, and she sat in the seat next to the aisle. The bus started to get a little stuffy. She was pretty. She wore a green dress with flowers below her neck. Blond hair bounced down and around her shoulders. She used little, if any, makeup. Across her forehead sweat beads formed.

"Are your parents still in New Jersey?"

"No, my father is dead."

"I'm sorry to hear that."

"My mother lives with me in Saltillo."

"What kind of research do you do in Saltillo?"

"I don't anymore." There was a tone of sorrow in her voice.

"Oh, what do you do now?"

"I run the family business," she said rather frankly.

"And that is…?"

"If you're really interested, we can discuss it later." She returned to her reading.

I'd never been to Mexico before, and I wanted to enjoy it to the fullest. I spoke three or four sentences in Spanish. My mother tried hard to push me into taking languages when I was in high school. I didn't; I was more interested in gymnastics and playing the drums. There I was in Mexico where gymnastics and drum playing profited me little. To tell the truth I did not play all that well.

The bus finally arrived in Monterrey. The tour guide explained to us the good and bad of being in this part of Mexico. All I remember is: careful what you drink and watch out for the little kids who will steal you blind.

As we walked down the aisle Lou Ann said to me, "There are better and cheaper places to stay than the tour company provides." She told me the names of two or three.

"Will I see you again?" I asked.

"Yes, I'll contact you in the next couple of days. Just enjoy your stay in Monterrey."

"I think I'll like it here."

Lou Ann got off the bus ahead of me. I took my luggage from underneath the bus. The sun was high in the sky, and it was already hot. I felt the sweat running down my back. I looked up and down the street looking for the places to stay Lou Ann suggested. Was I surprised when an old army jeep drove up in front of the bus? A young Mexican soldier in dress uniform got out and helped Lou Ann with her baggage. She got in the jeep, and they drove off down the street. The tour guide said the bus would leave the next day at six in the afternoon.

Monterrey, Mexico is a huge modern city, on the plain at the foot of large mountains. I saw people everywhere. At first I wondered if I were really in Mexico; it seemed like one more big city in the U.S. A boy of about ten came up and offered to take my luggage. I asked him if he knew the location of the Hotel Amigo. He shook his head yes, and then he motioned for me to follow him.

We walked three blocks from the bus terminal and turned right down what looked like an alley. At that point I knew I was in Mexico. Dirty, shabby-dressed kids played in the street. About half way down the alley a sign hung from the store front, Hotel Amigo. If Lou Ann hadn't recommended it, I would not have stayed there. The boy stopped out in front and put my baggage on the sidewalk. I handed him three dollars; at that point I only had US dollars. He grabbed the money and took off up the alley. It was as if he was out of his territory, and he knew it.

I picked up my luggage and went inside. The lobby was spacious and well lit. A man in an army uniform sat behind the counter. He jumped to attention. "Aw, senor, I've been expecting you."

"You have?" I asked.

"Si, Senora Lou Ann, told us you would probably be here and for us to have a nice room waiting for you."

"I suspect you just happen to have one nice room left?"

"Si, senor," he replied, with a smile all across his face.

Five men sat on the floor in the lobby. They were either shining their boots, or they were polishing their rifles. All wore army uniforms. Two were Mexicans, one black, one from Europe, one Japanese or Chinese.

"What's with the artillery?" I asked.

"We are mercenarios. We work for La Senora Lou Ann."

"Mercenaries?" I asked. "What's going on here?"

"You rest. La Senora will explain all to you." He handed me a key and pointed upstairs.

The key had a five on it. I reached for my luggage when one of the soldiers hopped up and took my luggage. He motioned for me to follow him. We went up the stairs to the next floor. He stopped in front of room five. He opened the door and led me into what was one of the nicest rooms I ever stayed in. A mural of Napoleon Bonaparte leading his army covered one entire wall.

"I think you will like this room," the soldier said.

"You speak English?" I asked.

"Yes. I am from Germany. My name is Hans. I enlisted three years ago. It was the best thing I ever did. English is the official language of our army. La Senora Lou Ann is one of a kind. She will take good care of you. You'll like her. Listen to her offer carefully."

"Offer?"

"Yes. She will make you a good offer. It is difficult for her to find good officers. It is not hard to get men to enlist. The pay is great. Many will willingly die for the money. She knows it is hard to find men who will not only follow orders but who will think when the going gets tough."

I thanked Hans, and he left. I looked around the room. It was immaculate. I suppose the sheets alone were worth more than any other room I ever stayed in. They were blue and made of either silk or satin; I couldn't tell the difference.

Someone knocked on the door. "Come in," I said.

A soldier pushed in a tray of food fit for a king. It contained three meats, two vegetables, four fruits, and a small piece of cake. The champagne floated in ice cold water. "From La Senora Lou Ann," the soldier said. He turned and marched out.

I could only imagine what her offer would be.

I slept well that night. There was absolute silence and absolute darkness. I woke up late the next morning. I almost forgot I was in Mexico. I got up and opened the thick curtain. Sunlight flooded in like a dam had burst. The room did not have a telephone or a TV or a radio. It was a place to think, and I thought. I wondered what I was doing there in such a room in Monterrey, Mexico. I wondered what the future held. I wondered what Senora Lou Ann planned for me.

I was hungry, but I decided to take a shower. The shower stall was the largest I'd ever seen. It had enough room for four people to dance. It had a built in stool at the end. I took off my clothes and threw them on the bed. I adjusted the water just the way I like it. I got in and began to lather up.

The glass door opened and in stepped La Senora Lou Ann. She was naked to the butt. I must have looked totally surprised, because I was.

"This is the first test I put my men through before I offer them a leadership position in my army," she said.

"Test?" I asked.

"Yes, see if you can keep your hands off me while we finish our showers." She picked up the soap and began to lather her body.

I looked her up and down. She was one sexy lady. I won't share my thoughts here with you. They were strong, but I just continued to soap and lather.

"Wash my back, would you, please," she said.

"Sure." I swallowed hard.

She rinsed off and got out of the shower stall. I could hear her toweling. I stayed in the shower, hoping she would leave, or at least have clothes on when I got out. I turned the water off and stepped out to discover she was gone. I was glad.

Lou Ann left a note for me on the bed. It read, "Meet me at the tourist bus stop at noon." It was only eight-thirty. I decided to get dressed, go out for breakfast, and walk around until noon. How could a family business be involved with mercenaries? I sure wanted to ask Lou Ann that question.

I walked up to the bus stop around eleven forty-five. I didn't see Lou Ann. About five minutes later an army jeep drove up with Lou Ann in the front seat, a handsome soldier driving.

"Get in!" she said, almost like an order.

"At your service, La Senora."

We drove out of town onto the plain and up into the mountains. I got a real panoramic view of the city. It was much larger than I thought, and beautiful. A river ran under the road as we passed between two mountains. The bridge was modern and impressive. Not a word was spoken until we got to our destination. It was an army camp almost at the top of one of the mountains.

A barricade blocked the entrance into the camp. Two soldiers in dress uniforms stood at attention. One saluted and opened the way for us to pass. The driver returned the salute. At once I could tell we had entered a serious army base, everything shined or painted. A modern tank decorated the marching field. A group of soldiers ran pass doing their daily PT.

We stopped in front of a two-story building. It looked like it could be the headquarters. I sat there until Lou Ann told me what to do.

"Get out and follow us. I have another test for you," she said.

"How do you know that I am even interested in whatever you are doing?" I asked.

"I don't, and I don't care until I know you are qualified."

"When will you know?"

"Soon, very soon."

She led me into the building and into a classroom. She told me to sit down at one of the desks. She gave me some sheets of paper and two pencils. I felt like I was back in high school. "This is a written test. If I were you, I'd do my very best."

"Or what, you won't let me join your little army?"

The test consisted of three parts: an essay section dealing with international politics, one where geometrical patterns were matched, and one with some math problems. I thought I did pretty well.

Lou Ann returned to the classroom. An older man in a perfect uniform followed her. I could tell right away he had to be in charge, under Lou Ann.

"This is General Martin Mitchell. He is over our entire army. I recruited him from our own CIA. He is the soldier's soldier."

"General."

"Welcome. We hope you have what we're looking for."

"And just what is that?"

"Officer material, the ability to lead soldiers into war."

"Wait a minute, general. Who said I want to join your army and lead men into war?"

"Nobody. We have not invited you yet. Let me see your test. It is a big part of how we detect what we need."

"I don't especially care about world politics."

"Neither do I," replied the general. He took the paper and studied it for several minutes.

"Well?" Lou Ann asked.

The general studied my answers for awhile longer and then said, "Yes, he is what we are looking for. Let's see how he handles the third and last test."

"Let's give him a good lunch first."

"Sure, he'll need it."

They fed me a hearty lunch. I was curious to see what final test awaited me. I found out right after we ate. The general beckoned me to follow him outside. Lou Ann came along and seemed to enjoy letting the general take charge. A jeep waited outside with six older soldiers in army fatigues. The jeep pulled a covered trailer behind it. I couldn't tell if it was empty or not. The soldiers all stood at attention.

The general looked at me and said, "I'm going to blindfold you now, and then we'll take you for a ride. These soldiers will assist you, just in case you don't want to take a ride."

I raised my hands in surrender and turned around so he could put the blindfold on. "I'll gladly go along for the ride." Again, I was curious to see what this was all about. I have to admit that I also was starting to get a little scared.

One of the soldiers helped me into the jeep. I could not see a thing. I didn't know who else got in the jeep. Somebody started up the jeep, and we drove off. We crossed a small bridge, and I heard the water below. It seemed like we were going up the mountain. It was further strange because nobody spoke the whole trip. I don't know how far we went but it seemed like a couple of hours.

Just before we stopped, I thought I heard what sounded like a donkey bray. It must have come from the trailer we were pulling. I had no idea what role a donkey could play in all of this. I was soon to find out. Not only did the donkey bray, but it began to kick and to make the trailer rock back and forth. I could feel the action as it affected the jeep.

The jeep finally stopped.   The general told me to take off the blindfold. It took me a few minutes to get my eyes adjusted to the sunlight. We stopped on a cliff overlooking a low valley. A river surged in the distance.

"What now?" I asked. I noticed the second jeep with three soldiers behind us.

"You get out," Lou Ann said.

I got out of the jeep. The general got out. Then Lou Ann got out; she was the only one not wearing a uniform. The other soldiers stayed put.

"Okay, here we are. Now what? What's with the donkey?" I asked.

"You noticed the mule?" the general commented.

"Keith," Lou Ann said. It was the first time she used my name. "This is the third test. I wish you the very best. I want badly for you to succeed here. We need you."

"Thank you. I am honored, I think." I smiled.

The general motioned to the soldiers in the back jeep. They got out and walked up to the trailer. The donkey started to bray and kick. It evidently did not like human beings.

Let me explain the third and final test. I know you don't know where you are. The trick is for you to find your way back to camp. There is, however, a catch to this."

"I bet there is," I replied.

"You have to bring the mule back with you."

I had no clue where the camp was. I had no clue how to handle the donkey. All I knew was that I was lost and was about to be tied up with a human-hating donkey.

The general motioned for the soldiers to get the donkey out of the trailer. They looked so cautious as they approached the trailer and handled the donkey. Lou Ann came around to observe. The soldiers had to force the donkey out. Once the donkey was out, they gave me the rope and stepped back.

The general and the soldiers started for the jeeps. The general smiled and saluted me. "I hope to see you in camp within the next twenty-four hours. This is your last test, and we actually hope you pass."

Lou Ann stepped toward me. She stood between me and the donkey. She kissed me on the cheek. "I hope you pass, too. You will make a handsome officer in our army."

I pulled on the rope. The donkey reared up its back legs and began kicking. One hoof hit Lou Ann in her stomach and the other on her forehead. Lou Ann fell to the ground. She was unconscious. I dropped the rope and ran over to Lou Ann. The donkey ran off. The general and the soldiers saw what happened and rushed to check Lou Ann.

Lou Ann's skull was fractured, and blood ran from her mouth. "She is alive," the general said, "but barely. We have to get her to the hospital." He pointed to one of the soldiers. "Radio for a helicopter ASAP!"

"Yes, sir." The soldier saluted and grimaced as he looked down at Lou Ann.

The general looked up at me. "If she dies, you die, my friend."

"It was an accident," I muttered.

"I don't give a damn, you jack ass. If she dies, you die."

I felt so helpless. "What can I do?"

"Nothing. I will give you three days head start. If she dies, I will turn my whole army loose to hunt you down. We will find you, and we will kill you." He threw me a set of keys and said, "Take a jeep and go hide somewhere, anywhere. I will give you a chance to protect yourself."

"Look, general, it was an accident."

One of the soldiers pointed his rifle at me. The general said something to him in Spanish. The soldier fired a shot that creased my leg. "The next bullet will be between your eyes. Now get out of my sight. Three days, mind you, three days."

I didn't argue further. I took the jeep and drove off. I heard a helicopter in the distance.

Somehow I found my way down into Monterrey and to the Hotel Amigo. I quickly put my things together. I stopped once to find out how to get to the airport. I bought a ticket to Atlanta, Georgia. Once in Atlanta I decided what my plan would be: I would hideout somewhere in the hills around Guntersville Lake. That area contains lots of hilly wooden areas with lots of places to hide.

I decided to call my sister. I didn't want her worrying about me.

"Something has come up. I have an opportunity I can't let slip," I told her.

"What's wrong, Keith?" I could tell she was worried. "The FBI is looking for you."

"The FBI?" I asked. "Why?"

"They think you were kidnapped in Mexico. Somebody on a tour bus reported you as missing."

"How did you find out that information?"

"They called here yesterday asking about you."

"What did you tell them?"

"That you were traveling south, going to Mexico. I didn't even know you had gotten to Monterrey."

"Listen, everything is going to be alright. I just need to hide for awhile. Don't tell the FBI that I called. I'm not totally sure what this is all about."

I took a bus from the airport to downtown Atlanta. I hailed a taxi and located a cheap off-brand car rental business. I rented a car and headed north to Rome, Georgia where I got another rental car. I also bought a sleeping bag and a tent and other camping equipment. Then I crossed the Alabama state line and drove on to Guntersville. I bought some food and drinks. I drove into the wilderness as far as the car could take me. I drove the car off the road and hid it the best I could. Then I took out walking. I was looking for a nice but lonely water fall. I thought I remembered one in the area from my camping trips as a teenager.

About an hour before the sun set I found exactly what I needed. The waterfall was about thirty feet high. I could still see the cave behind the falling water. There was no sign of human activity anywhere around: footprints, trash, etc. I had only brought the sleeping bag and food after I hid the car. I would have to go back to the car the next day and get the rest of the things I brought.

I gathered wood and dry leaves and started a fire in the back of the cave. I wondered all along if Lou Ann died or was still alive. I wondered if the general and his soldiers would really come hunting for me. I realized they knew much more about hunting than I did about hiding. I wondered if I would die in the next several days. I stayed awake most of the night thinking and listening to the water fall outside the cave. The crickets were also loud that night. The light from the moon reflected off the water and every now and then formed a small rainbow. If my life had not been at stake, that could have been one of the most peaceful nights of my life.

The next morning I prepared a light breakfast and walked back to the car to get the rest of my supplies. I had a difficult time finding the car; I did a great job of hiding it. I tried to cover the car back the way I left it initially.

However, when I turned to start walking up to my waterfall, I was confronted by six men. One was a forest ranger, two local policemen, and three (I assumed) FBI agents. At least they were not soldiers from the general in Mexico.

"You're lucky we found you before the others did," one of the agents said.

"Is it that bad? Did Lou Ann die?"

"Oh, yes, the great La Senora Lou Ann is dead at last, and there is a world-wide contract out on you. You would not have had a chance."

"What happens now?"

"You're going to tell us what you know and what you saw in Mexico."

"Why do you care about those mercenaries?"

"That army of renegades only fights on the wrong side and for the right amount of cash. The general and his army, led by La Senora Lou Ann, have often even fought our own US Army. To say the least, they are not our allies."

"Then what happens to me?" I asked.

"Protective custody, better known as the witness protection program. We're going to find you a real nice waterfall and cave and stick you in there forever."

"You've been talking to my sister, haven't you?"

"Yes, we have."

The Witness as a Victim

Most people don't like to visit or even think about cemeteries, much less work in one. Old Benny had been in the burying business for over thirty years. There wasn't much he hadn't seen around cemeteries. He had observed with much distain the so-called progress in burying people. Even with new machines available to him, he still liked to dig graves with a shovel. It was the personal touch that mattered.

Old Benny lived in a redone barn among the trees in the back section of the cemetery. It had an indoor toilet and a fireplace. It still had the rafters in the ceiling. He was never alone. His many visitors included cats, snakes, bats, bugs, and rats. He liked every one of them and never made them feel unwelcome.

In the daytime the trees shaded the shack, and in the nighttime the darkness enclosed it and made it feel as sterile as the surgeon's scalpel. Death didn't frighten Old Benny; in fact, he welcomed it. Before he dug graves, he worked for one of the morticians in one of the nearby villages. He decided he'd rather bury dead bodies than work on them.

Behind the cemetery lived a band of Negroes whose ancestors had led a nomad life in the old country. About ten years earlier they settled on the land back of the cemetery. Old Benny had never had any trouble with any of them. Folks in town accused the blacks of being witches and practicing witchcraft. The Negroes, however, claimed that Benny conversed with ghosts inside the cemetery.

One night a cat scratched on the outside of Benny's door. Benny opened the door and let the cat come in. The cat was solid black, weighed about thirty pounds, and was a female. The cat meowed and purred and rubbed up against Benny's legs. Benny loved cats and was a sucker for a lonely stranger.

"Pretty cat, are you lost this time of night?"

The cat purred.

"Do you have a name?"

The cat looked up at Old Benny and stared as if to say, 'Of course, don't you have a name?'

"You are solid black, and you came on a full moon. I think I will call you Moonlight."

The cat meowed as if to approve of her new name.

"Are you hungry, Moonlight?"

Moonlight purred louder.

The old man filled a bowl with milk and fed the cat. Later he sat down in his rocker and picked up the picture of a dark-haired little girl. The girl was about nine-years-old. He kissed the picture and replaced it on the table. He opened an old blue-colored shawl and spread it across his legs. Just like most other nights, he fell asleep in the rocker. The next morning when he awoke, the cat was gone.

Earlier that night the Negroes had gathered beside a fresh grave in the cemetery. The aim was to dig up one fresh body and cut out the heart. An illness was sweeping the area that nobody seemed to have a cure. They needed a heart and the left little finger of one dead to concoct a remedy for their own ailing folk. They didn't want Old Benny to hear or to see them. Because of the ghosts they feared killing Benny.

Old Benny slept well that night. The next morning during his rounds in the cemetery he noticed the new grave was sinking at one end. He went for a shovel and a bucket of dirt to fill in the grave. Moonlight was waiting at the grave when he returned.

"There you are, Moonlight."

The cat didn't purr or meow. It just watched Old Benny fill in the grave.

"I wondered what happened to you last night."

Still Moonlight just sat there.

Benny waved at the cat and went on about his business.

Later that night there was the scratch again at the door. The moon was still full. Shadows danced among the trees. The wind whistled as it rushed here and there in the midst of the trees and the tombstones. The old man opened the door. For the second night the black cat wanted in.

"Back again tonight, huh, Moonlight?"

The black cat meowed and purred and rubbed against Benny's legs.

"Come in. Come in. I've got more milk for you."

Moonlight came into the room as if she belonged there.

Old Benny fetched her a bowl of milk. He watched as she licked up the milk. Finally, he sat down in his rocker. He spread the blue shawl over his legs and kissed the picture of the dark-haired girl. He replaced the picture on the table and was fast asleep. The next morning when he awoke, Moonlight was gone.

Later that day he noticed that same grave was again sinking. When he returned with his shovel and bucket of dirt, Moonlight was there again waiting for him. Beside the grave he dropped the shovel and put down the bucket. He reached over to pat Moonlight, but she moved away from him.

"Is it only when I have milk that we are friends?" he asked.

Moonlight moved further away from him and watched him.

Old Benny poured the dirt over the grave and filled in the sinking part. He wondered why the grave had sunk two days in a row. That was most unusual.

Moonlight meowed and hissed and scurried away.

"I bet I see you again tonight," Benny said, as he watched the cat vanish behind one of the large granite monuments.

Later that night Benny again heard the scratching at the door. He expected the cat and had a bowl of milk ready. When he opened the door, the cat scrambled into the room.

"What's gotten into you? You afraid of something?"

Moonlight stopped in front of the rocker and looked up at the picture of the dark-haired little girl. The old man placed the bowl on the floor. Moonlight drank all of the milk. Benny put the bowl in the sink. He sat down in his rocker, spread the shawl over both legs, kissed the picture of the little girl, and was about to go to sleep.

Moonlight jumped up on the shawl. She meowed and purred and rubbed her nose on his chin. The whiskers tickled the old man. He sneezed once or twice. He looked down at the cat and saw something for the first time. It was the eyes and the black hair that made him pick up the picture and look hard and scratch his bald head.

"No. It's my imagination. My tired eyes are playing tricks on me. That's what I get for getting old. I'm seeing things." He pushed the cat, and she jumped down on the floor. He picked up the picture and smiled. "My dear, Patsy, I love and miss you so." Tears ran down his face and wet his shirt. Finally, he fell asleep.

Moonlight jumped back up in the old man's lap. She purred and purred and kneaded the shawl. "My dear, dear father. If only I could tell you who I am. That will never happen, but I am here to save you from any misfortune." Moonlight jumped back down onto the floor and vanished into the darkness of the night.

Later that night the queen Negro and several of her court met behind one of the larger monuments to mix their concoction. They had a huge black pot. It was filled with herbs and minerals and secret ingredients. The queen cut one of the male's arms and dripped the blood into the pot.

"We are almost ready," the queen said, in a tone from the darkest secret part of Africa.

The others laughed and jumped up and down.

"Be quiet," the queen demanded. "We don't need that old man Benny out here with his ghosts, do we?"

"No," they all responded.

Sometime during the night Benny woke up and was hot. He dropped the shawl on the floor and went to open the window above the sink. Through the open window he was able to see shadows dancing on the monuments in the cemetery. 'What's that', he wondered. 'I better go check it out.'

The closer he got, the better he could see and hear. There was a strange humming sound and the clanging of the spoon and the pot. Finally, he could see plainly the queen and her court. She was stirring the pot, and the others were dancing in a circle around her. That humming sound he had heard came from two males who sat off from the circle humming.

'What are they doing?' Benny asked himself.

"Don't move," a deep voice spoke from behind old Benny.

Benny turned slightly and slowly to see a tall half naked black man.

"Let's go see the queen," he demanded in a husky tone.

"What are you folks up to?" Benny asked.

The black man did not answer. He pulled a long knife from his side and pushed Benny toward the fire and the group.

"Where did he come from?" the queen asked.

"I found him over behind those stones." The man pointed to the monuments where old Benny had been hiding.

"You're the ones who've been tampering with the graves?"

"Yes, but you'll never live to tell anyone," the queen replied.

"What are you up to? Why are you here in the cemetery?"

"The white man's sickness is about to kill all our people. I decided to kill many of those whites before they kill us all."

"You mean revenge?"

"No, I mean black magic," the queen laughed and began stirring the pot again. "Kill him, and we'll add him to the pot. That will make the curse even stronger."

Nobody noticed the big black cat as she drew closer and closer to the crowd. She stood up next to the fire and cast a huge monstrous shadow over the monuments. Then she let out this blood-boiling scream. All the black folks jumped in fear and pointed toward the shadow.

"Don't worry, my children," the queen said. "My magic is much stronger than that of the white man."

The cat screamed again. The shadow grew even larger and more frightening.

"Right now, throw the white man in the pot. His death will run away all our enemies."

Before anyone could touch old Benny, the cat turned into four ghosts and began haunting the blacks. That was more than any of them could stand. They turned over the pot to put out the fire. The fire sizzled and smoldered. The blacks escaped in all directions. It was impossible to even consider catching up with a single one of them because they left there in such a hurry. Monstrous shadows? Maybe. But not ghosts. There are limits to all a culture can endure.

Old Benny walked back to the barn in a daze. He thought surely he was still asleep and only dreaming. Moonlight was in the room next to the rocker when he entered. She was waiting on him. He thought she wanted some milk. He prepared the milk and put it on the floor. Moonlight drank none of it.

"Are you not hungry tonight?" Benny was tired from the excitement.

Moonlight rubbed up against his legs and purred and meowed.

Benny sat down in the rocker. He left the shawl on the floor. He picked up the picture and kissed the little girl. Moonlight jumped up in the old man's lap. Again, he noticed the cat's black hair and her eyes. There was something familiar about Moonlight. Then the cat shook her head to one side and looked up at old Benny. Benny recalled that that was just like what Patsy used to do with her long black hair.

"Patsy, I love you and miss you so much. I am having visions now. This old man is getting crazier and crazier."

Moonlight snuggled up against Benny. For a moment the man was holding his little girl. Tears ran down his face. The excitement had left him tired and confused. Moonlight settled down in his lap and kneaded his legs ever so gently. The old man fell asleep, and his hand fell to his side. He dropped the picture, and it broke the glass into several pieces.

A peaceful and serene smile covered Benny's face. His heartbeat slowed down to almost nothing. Then it stopped completely. Moonlight jumped down on the floor. About six minutes later two black cats ran out the door into the still darkness.

The U-Haul Express

The driver of the U-Haul pulled off Highway 12 into Shadow Memory Gardens. He immediately switched off his head lights. The only light was the dim porch light in front of the office building and the moon peeping through the think cover of clouds. He could see the old dry fountain and the road as it circled the fountain. His mother and daddy were both buried in the Garden of Prayer across from the pond. However, it was not his parents that brought him to the cemetery in the middle of the night driving a U-Haul.

Out in the middle of the cemetery the truck could not be seen from the highway. In the rider's seat sat the owner of a real estate firm in Cope City, Alabama. He owned and ran a boating firm on the Warrior River and on Smith Lake. However, it was neither real estate nor boats that brought this man to Shadow Memory Gardens in the wee hours of the morning.

These two men were in high school together. One was successful, but the other it seemed was always getting them both into some kind of trouble. They were highly patriotic and served in the army together. Both always wanted more money. Often they got into some scrapes that were way over their heads. This caper was certainly one of them.

"Are you sure they are going to meet us here?"

"I'm sure. At least if they know what's good for them."

The week before an old army buddy was in town and took them out to eat. He said he had a business proposition to share that involved a U-Haul truck and the local cemetery. He assured them the pay was good and would definitely cover the danger. It was the danger part that concerned both men. All they were told is that it involved a project to improve conditions in the United States.

"I think I like working in Arkansas better than in Alabama. At least there I always knew what I was getting myself into. I pulled some stupid stunts before I came back home. I sure hope this is not another one of them."

Johnny Fulgrim laughed.

"What's so funny?" asked Matt Johnson.

"This is backwards. Usually the hearse brings dead people here to be buried. Here we are in a U-Haul to dig up live people. I never heard of such a thing. How do these folk survive under the ground?"

"Do you believe what they're doing is right, or are you in this just for the money?"

"Well," he stopped a little to think. "I certainly like the money, but in a way I think I am behind the cause. We DO need a change in this country. I'm tired of our trying to police the whole world. It's like every recent president has gotten us into some military quarrel somewhere in the world. Why can't we just mind our own business?"

The moon broke through the clouds. The two men heard an engine start up. It sounded like it was moving toward them. They got out of the truck. Soon they saw a back hoe in the moon light. It looked like a giant insect coming after them. Their first impulse was to flee and not look back. They regained their confidence before the back hoe arrived.

The two men walked off the paved road onto the grass. They were standing in front of a black granite private mausoleum. The back hoe stopped beside the truck. A large black man got down from the back hoe. He motioned the two white men to the side and went around to the back of the mausoleum. The name on the front of the mausoleum was the same as the city's mayor: Cartwright.

"I need to check the air supply and the platform stability before I open this huge grave."

"How long have they been in the ground?"

"Five days, but they had plenty of food and water, and I dug them a really big hole."

"How many of them come through this cemetery in a month's time?"

The black man said, "We hide between thirty and forty soldiers a month."

It had rained a little earlier that afternoon, and the ground was wet but not really muddy. The black man acted like he knew exactly what he was doing and in fact had done this many times in the past. He moved a layer of sod that looked fake at closer inspection and said "okay?" into a pipe coming up out of the ground. A hearty "okay" came back from the grave below.

A car drove by out on the highway. They all felt a little uneasy.

"Does anyone have any notion of what is going on out here in this cemetery?"

"Not a soul, as far as I know," said the black man. "Not even those who work here."

Once he moved the layer hiding the hiding place, one could hear a small engine grinding below. It was pulling fresh air into the space below. Listening closely the men heard the breathing and some activity of the soldiers. They were restless and were ready to be out of the ground. Even trained soldiers can only take so much.

As the black man and the two white men stood over the grave of the living, it started to mist. A cool breeze swept through the monuments. Every now and then a loose flower would scoot past their working area. The nervous sweat on all the men dried and then evaporated. It was scary and exciting to be working in a cemetery in the middle of the night.

The black man went back to the back hoe and drove it over to the grave. He cautiously opened the hole before he removed the wooden plank covering the soldiers. A host of "thanks" came up from the foreigners. They all spoke with a strong accent. A reeking odor of feces and urine belched up into the fresh air.

The black man threw down a rope ladder which he brought over from the back hoe. The men below covered some of their trash with dirt. They gathered their supplies. Not one of them looked to be over twenty-five years old.

"Hurry, hurry," the black man exclaimed.

"Is there a time constraint?" one of the white men asked.

"No," replied the black man.

The officer in charge shook his head and definitely made it known they were in a hurry to get to their next destination.

There were six soldiers in all. They climbed up the rope ladder, each carrying a weapon, ammunition, and explosives. Without saying another word, they got in the back of the U-Haul truck. The black man closed the door and checked the air hole in the side of the truck. He smacked the back door letting those inside know they were about to pull out of the cemetery.

Matt and Johnny stood there and glared at the black man. "Okay, now what?"

"And what about the money?" said the black man.

"That's right."

"Take these men to Lake Warrior where there will be another U-Haul truck waiting for them," the black man said. "You will be paid there, as we promised, after these soldiers are safely on their way to the next cemetery."

"Just exactly who are these men? I know they are soldiers."

"Do you really want to know, or do you just want to do the job and get the money?"

"I want to know."

"They are terrorists from the Middle East."

The two white men looked at each other.

"Just exactly where are they headed?"

"To the White House, of course!"

"Of course, where else would terrorists go?"

Before Johnny and Matt actually drove the truck out of the cemetery, the rain started to pour down. They had to stop and change a flat tire on the truck. Evidently they picked up a nail earlier in the evening. A police car rode by the cemetery. The officer flashed his light out over the grounds of the cemetery, but he noticed nothing.

The U-Haul pulled out on Highway 12 headed for its destination. Inside were six living soldiers from the city of the dead intent on killing their targets in the city of the living.

P O Box 454

At two o'clock in the morning everyday Grant Horton visited the post office. He grunted and complained as he went in, and he sang and rejoiced as he went out. Only a few folks knew about this strange habit. I was one of the few because I was his grandson. Papa, as we called him, had retired from the local police department. He was shot in the chest the year he retired.

Papa served this city thirty years without any physical injury, but on his last car chase a bank robber shot him after Papa forced the car off the highway almost at the northern city limit sign. Papa was able to return fire. He shot the robber in the head, and the man died in the hospital two hours later. Papa spent six months in the hospital during which time he suffered three near-death operations.

My family moved back to my Dad's home to take care of Papa. Clay Horton, my Dad, was a policeman also. He was killed in action before I finished high school. Papa never got over Dad's death. But, wait, I'm getting ahead of myself in telling this story. Let's get back to Papa.

I remember Papa taking me fishing the very first time. I was only six years old. I didn't know how to fish or how to bait the hook or anything about fishing. Papa taught me all I now know.

"That worm won't bite you," Papa assured me.

"It's gooey," I replied.

"Do you want to catch a fish?"

"Yes, sir."

"Then stick that hook into that worm, and let's get to fishing."

I did as Papa told me. I now know that I did not do it right. The worm just flopped on the end of my hook. However, as soon as I tossed the line in the water, the cork went for the bottom, and the pole fell into the water. Papa grabbed it and handed it back to me.

"Now you bring that there fish out of the water and land it here at our feet."

I tried and I tried. I dropped the pole again. It sank in the water. Papa missed as he tried to grab it again. I knew I had done wrong. I started crying. Papa knelt down beside me and put me on his leg. I continued to cry. Papa wiped the tears from my face.

"It's alright; you'll catch the next one."

"You think so?"

"I know so."

Years later when I needed reassuring and loving, I just recalled Papa's words, "It's alright; you'll catch the next one." You know what? I did catch the next one, and Papa was there to congratulate me and tell me he told me so. Papa was a good man. He was a wonderful grandfather. I really miss him.

I remember when I was in the cub scouts and had to make a model race car. Papa was there to guide me. He was the most patient man on earth.

"Do you think this car can win the race Saturday?"

"No, I don't think so; I know so."

"Papa, how do you know?"

"Because I'm an old man and just know those kinds of things. When you get older, you'll know those kinds of things, too."

We worked that entire week on that model race car. Papa gave me all his time. I picked out the color I wanted to paint my car. I picked out the wood. I polished the wheels, and I put it all together. When Saturday finally came, we were ready. Papa and I arrived at the fairgrounds about an hour early. We wanted to make sure things were ready for that race.

"Just take your car to the top of the hill and let it go. Then watch it race down the hill. I will be waiting at the bottom to catch it and take you to get your prize."

I did as Papa told me. When I let it go, the wheels stuck and stopped the car two feet out of the starting gate. I didn't win first place. I didn't win second place. I didn't even win third place. I didn't even finish the race. I knew I had done wrong. I started crying, and Papa knelt down beside me. He put me on his leg. I continued to cry. Papa wiped those tears from my face.

"It's alright; you'll win the next time."

"You really thing so."

"I know so."

Years later after Papa died and I needed reassuring and loving, I just recalled Papa's line: "It's alright; you'll win next time." You know what? I did win the next time. I entered the school spelling bee and won. Papa was there to congratulate me and tell me he told me so. Papa was a good man. He was the best grandfather a kid ever had. I really miss him.

I remember when Papa was shot and almost died. I went to the hospital every day, but I was too young to visit the intensive care ward. Finally, Papa demanded that they let me go see him. Papa looked older than ever before. He was more concerned about me than about himself.

"How are you?" he asked.

"I'm fine, Papa. I'm really sorry I haven't been to see you, but they wouldn't let me in."

"I know; that's why I threw a fit and demanded they let you in." He chuckled a little.

"Papa, I wish you weren't here. I miss seeing you."

I'll never forget what happened next. Papa started to cry.

"What's the matter, Papa?"

"I'm going to die."

I wiped the tears from Papa's face. "I don't think so."

"You don't think so?"

"No, Papa, I know you're not going to die."

I sat down on the edge of the bed. I hugged Papa and kissed him. He held my hand and told me he loved me and that he was proud of me. Papa was a good man. He was one of a kind and the best grandfather in the whole wide world. I really miss him.

I remember years later when my Dad was killed. One night he was chasing a man who had raped this little girl. He followed the man into an empty office building. There were no lights, and my Dad had dropped his flashlight in the chase. The man was waiting for my Dad behind one of the doors. When Dad entered the room, the man hit him over the head with a steel beam. My Dad died before the ambulance arrived.

My mother did not accept his death well at all. However, it was Papa who took it worse. He went into a deep depression. I tried to console both my mother and Papa. Mother got a little better with time. Papa just got worse and worse. I visited him often at his house. I saw him many times crying and breathing with effort due to the bullet wound.

"Papa, how are you today?"

"I read in the paper where they let the man who killed you Dad out of prison."

"I know," I said. "How could they do that?"

"Some damn lawyer found some way to sway the jury to find him innocent."

I had only heard Papa curse one other time. "What will happen now?"

"Nothing," Papa said. "Unless we do something."

"Papa, what do you mean?"

"I am a professional policeman, but now the time is here to take the law into our own hands."

"Do you really mean that?"

"If I were able, I would kill that murderer myself."

"Papa, would you?"

"Yes, I would."

Papa didn't tell me I ought to kill my Dad's killer. He did put the idea in my head. 'If Papa would do it,' I thought, 'then I need to do it.' Papa was a good man. He was the best grandfather in the world. I really miss him. The next day I took Dad's police revolver and set out to kill his killer.

I found the man home with his wife and small daughter. I knocked on the door. When the man opened the door, I kicked it and forced my way in.

"Who are you? What do you want?"

"I'm going to kill you, you bastard." I pointed the revolver at him.

His wife started screaming. That made me really nervous. I yelled for her to shut up. She just screamed louder. I shot the man in the head point blank. I got blood all over me. His wife was carrying the little girl. She ran at me. Her action scared me, and I shot her in the heart. The bullet went through the baby's head first. There I stood with three dead bodies. I was seventeen years old.

They tried me as an adult for murder. I got three life time sentences without parole. My friends and even my family were shocked and ashamed of what I had done. All forsook me. All except for Papa. I was sent away to the state prison. Papa was not able to come visit me.

Two years later Papa died. Of course, I was not able to attend the funeral. In my dreams and in my thoughts, I can still hear Papa say two things. "It's alright; you'll catch the next one." "It's alright; you'll win the next time."

While Papa was still alive, he and I wrote daily. Everybody tried to get him to leave me alone and let me suffer for what I had done. Papa didn't do that.

At two o'clock in the morning everyday for those two years Grant Horton visited the post office. He grunted and complained as he went in, and he sang and rejoiced as he went out. Only a few folks knew about this strange habit. I was one of the few because I was his grandson.

Papa was a good man. He was the best grandfather in the whole world. I really miss him. I wish he were here to wipe my tears away.

Alabama Fever

"Momma, momma, wake up. We've got news about Brad."

"Brad? Did you say Brad was home?"

"No, momma. We got a letter at the post office today."

"A letter? A letter from Brad, did you say?"

The clouds, fluffy and grayish, floated across the window. The sun was setting beyond the rolling hills, the valleys full of jumping shadows. Leaves of all colors covered the ground. A flock of geese flew overhead and landed in the lake at the end of the field. A deer pranced across the front yard.

Corina turned from the window and walked back over to the bed where momma lay, her head propped up on two pillows. Corina wiped sweat from momma's forehead. Momma had a fever on and off for over a week. Momma's eyes were black and sunken.

"Momma, Brad's coming home."

"Dear, did you say Brad's coming home?"

"Yes, momma. He's on his way to Washington DC. He's getting some kind of a medal, and the president is giving it to him."

"I'm sorry, dear. I don't understand what you're saying. Please, say it again."

"Brad is on his way to Washington. He's getting the highest medal the military gives; it's called the Congressional Medal of Honor. Can we go see him?"

"Us, go to Washington? Nobody in our family's ever been out of Alabama except Brad. I bet he doesn't need us there."

"But, momma, I'm sure he would want us there."

Momma glanced over at the mantel above the fireplace. There was a picture of Brad in his dress uniform, his Green Beret on his head. That picture had served as the center of attention for the past six years. The entire family almost worshipped it. Nobody in the family had served in the army since the Civil War. In fact the cemetery in back was full of dead Confederate soldiers, many from their family.

Momma looked down at the quilt laid over her. "My grandmother made this quilt when she was just a little girl, and she gave it to my mother. My mother added to it and gave it to me when I was sixteen. Over the years I've added to it, and I will give it to you soon, my dear."

"It is beautiful, momma, and I truly want it for my very own."

"My point, dear, is that this family is Alabama, and that is all we know. It is all we really need to know. Nobody but Brad has left Alabama. That is okay for him, but it is not for the rest of us. We are Alabama, and that is all we need."

"I understand, momma. It's just that Brad is being honored."

"We will see him here with all his honors. He is a good boy, and we can honor him right here in Alabama."

"Yes, ma'am."

"Dear, bring me a drink of water. It is so hot, and I am so tired."

Someone knocked on the front door. "Anybody home?"

It was Miss Brenda Perkins. She taught at the school the other side of the hollow. She also taught voice lessons. Music was her first love. She came from the south side of Birmingham. She dreamed of making it big on Broadway. Everyone knew she sang like a bird. She liked Corina from the first. She had her favorite students and treated them special.

"Come in, Miss Brenda," Corina invited.

Brenda Perkins entered the room. Corina thought she looked like a picture from one of those fashion magazines from way up north. Every hair on her head was in place. Her dress looked like she'd just ironed it. Her face was white and pretty; she looked like she avoided the sun.

Corina, on the other hand, looked more like an orphan. She could not remember the last new dress she got. Momma made most of them by hand, and they were hard to come by. Her hair was combed, but tugging and pulling on momma caused many hairs to be out of place. Her face was dark brown and sort of plain. She spent lots of time outside working in the garden and doing other chores.

"How's your momma?" Brenda asked.

"I heard you," momma said. "And I can still talk."

"Yes, ma'am. I just didn't want to bother you."

"She's been arguing with me. I hope that means she's better." Corina answered.

"Corina, I really came by to see if you planned to enter the singing contest next Saturday over at the Methodist Church?"

"Miss Brenda, I don't think so."

"You should; you're a good singer. Tell me why you shouldn't go?"

"Well, because momma needs me, and because my brother Brad's coming home."

"Oh, the good looking one in the uniform over the mantel?"

"That's him. He's getting some big medal in Washington DC. The president is going to give it to him personally."

"The President of the United States?"

"That's right. The President of the United States."

Brenda Perkins was awed that someone from the backwoods of Alabama could end up getting a medal from the president of the United States. "What did he do to earn that?"

Corina motioned toward the door. "Let's go outside and let momma rest."

"Okay, then you can tell me."

Corina placed the pitcher of fresh water on the stand beside momma's bed. "We will be right back, momma. We're going outside for some fresh air. If you need me, remember to ring the bell. I can hear it."

Outside the cabin the air smelled much fresher. The sun smiled down on the earth. The wind ruffled both ladies' hair. A dear and a rabbit ran across the front yard. They sat in a swing under a big oak tree.

"Well," Brenda Perkins urged Corina.

Corina told Miss Perkins Brad's story. He'd taken a patrol out to check a building for enemy soldiers when they came under heavy fire. Two of his men were wounded and one killed. Brad and his men were pinned down, surrounded on all sides. Another of his men was hit by enemy fire. Realizing the severity and almost hopeless situation, Brad left his men in an attempt to get to higher ground where he could fire down on the enemy. He managed to crawl to a nearby building and from the roof to hold off the enemy until help arrived. In the process he received two flesh wounds to his legs and broke his left wrist. While he was in the hospital, his commanding officer sent a recommendation in for Brad to get the Medal of Honor. The request was granted, and the President of the United States was going to give the medal personally to him.

"Wow, a real war hero," Brenda Perkins commented.

"We are proud, but we're really glad he's coming home," Corina exclaimed.

"When can I meet him?" Miss Brenda asked, a little flirtation in her voice.

"I'm not really sure when he's coming. He wasn't sure what all the army had for him to do or when he could leave Washington DC."

Corina and Brenda left the swing and walked toward the barn. The chickens cackled and parted left and right. Brenda held her nose as they went pass the hog pen where three fat pigs wallowed in the mud. A lone goat stood on a tree stump in front of the barn and just stared at them as they entered. Brenda liked horses. Although Corina's folk had only one ole mare, Brenda liked to pet it and to talk to it.

"I'm going to have me a horse one of these days," Miss Perkins said, rubbing the nose of the old mare.

"Is that before or after you become a famous singer on Broadway?" Corina asked.

"I don't care as long as I have one."

Corina heard momma ringing the bell from inside the cabin. "That's momma ringing her bell; I need to go check on her."

"I hope she gets to feeling better. I'll see you later. Remember: I want to meet Brad as soon as possible." Miss Perkins giggled softly as she walked away.

The next morning, momma didn't look better. In fact, she looked much worse. There was a doctor about twenty miles away. Everybody liked Dr. Robert Fraley. He had only been to momma's house once before when Brad was young and nearly cut his leg off with an ax. By now the good doctor was getting up in years. Corina walked the mile to their nearest neighbor and used the phone to call Dr. Fraley. He assured Corina that he would be by to see momma by dark.

Dr. Fraley finally arrived late that afternoon. Corina and Brenda Perkins were caring for momma and watching for the doctor. Corina called Miss Perkins while she was at the neighbor's and asked her to come over.

Corina and Brenda met the doctor as he got out of his old Ford pickup. Despite his age he still walked erect and briskly. There was an air of knowledge and authority that came along with him. He carried his medical bag as if it contained the most precious jewels in the whole world.

"How is your momma?" the doctor asked.

"About the same," Corina replied. "We sure are glad to see you."

"Who is this other pretty lady?" he asked.

Corina introduced Dr. Fraley and Brenda Perkins to each other. The doctor was glad to know that Miss Perkins was from Birmingham, his hometown. They chatted about some of the niceties and modern gadgets one could find in Birmingham.

After some fifteen minutes the doctor said, "Ladies, excuse me, but I must see about the patient." He left them outside and went into the cabin to examine momma.

Thirty minutes later the doctor stuck his head out the door and called the two ladies into the cabin. "Let me ask you a few questions, Corina?"

"Yes, sir."

"Has momma said anything about a metal taste in her mouth?"

"Yes, she frequently claims the water has something in it. I just thought it was because the well was so old."

"Has she complained of being tired, cold, and not able to get enough sleep?"

"That's why she has the quilt over her when it so nice and warm in here."

"Have her legs bothered her?"

"I have seen her often reaching down and rubbing them?"

"Has she been confused or forgetful?"

"Yes, I had a hard time explaining to her that Brad is coming home?"

"Is he still in the army?"

Corina explained to the doctor about Brad's getting the Medal of Honor, which impressed him, especially the part about the President of the United States.

"Have momma's hands or feet been swelling?"

"Her hands; she's even dropped a few things because of it."

"Has there been any blood in her urine?"

"I noticed a little the other day when I emptied her pot, but I thought she probably rubbed herself too hard."

"Well, let's step outside and talk a little bit more," the doctor said.

The air outside was sweeter and fresher than inside the cabin. The sun was going down behind the hills and the trees. There was an orange glow all across the sky. Peace and calmness should have been the words of the day, but they weren't.

Corina sensed that momma's condition was worse than she thought. "How is she, Doctor Fraley?"

"I'm afraid she's not doing so well."

"What's wrong with her?" Brenda Perkins asked.

"I'm not rightly sure, but I think she is suffering from kidney failure."

Corina had no idea what that meant, but the words scared her. "Is she going to die?"

"I hope not," the doctor offered. "We need to get her to a hospital in Birmingham so she can see somebody a lot smarter than me."

Corina looked frustrated. "She won't go. She won't leave this cabin. Brad is coming so she thinks she has to stay right here."

The doctor walked on toward his old Ford pickup, his medical bag swinging at his side. He looked tired and older that when he first arrived. He spit the end of his toothpick in the grass. "Before long we won't need to ask her."

"Why is that?" Corina asked.

"At the stage she's in, she'll slip in and out of consciousness or go into a coma soon."

"I wish Brad were here," Corina said. "He'd know what to do."

"Well, we can't wait for him to get here; we need to do something now. I'll be back tomorrow. You have her things ready to go. I'll contact a doctor I know and the hospital in Birmingham to make all the arrangements."

"Okay, Doctor Fraley." Corina fought back her tears.

The good doctor got in his truck and drove away, smoke puffing out the muffler.

The sun settled behind the hills and trees, and darkness settled over the barnyard and over the cabin. Corina wished she could just go to sleep and wake up the next morning to find all her worries and troubles vanished. She and Miss Brenda went back to the swing. For a few minutes they were silent and just rocked in the swing.

"Everything is going to be okay," Miss Brenda reassured Corina. "Momma is strong and stubborn. She's got a lot of time left here on this ole earth."

"I hope so, Miss Brenda; I really hope so."

The two ladies went into the cabin to check on momma. She was asleep. Brenda Perkins decided to leave for her home. She assured Corina she would return the first thing in the morning. Corina thanked her for all her help and concern.

Corina sat in the rocking chair beside momma's bed. She read to momma from the Bible and then from a novel by Patsy Moreland, and then she sang some songs for her. Momma must have slept the whole time; she never responded to Corina. Corina got up and fetched some cool water from the sink and a clean wash cloth and began to bathe momma. There was a foul odor in the cabin that she just could not get rid of. She fluffed momma's pillow and tucked the quilt in around momma and kissed her goodnight.

The cabin had two other rooms; one was Brad's bedroom and the other was where Corina kept her things and slept. She used to share that room with momma. With momma in the bed in the main room of the cabin, Corina felt guilty over her childish feelings when she had to share not only the room but the bed also.

Corina wondered how long it would be before Brad would get home. She needed him at that moment, not some future time. Corina almost slept in the rocking chair but decided to go to bed and get a better night's rest. She should feel better in the morning in order to get momma ready to go to the hospital.

She lay in the bed for some time trying to read more of the Patsy Moreland novel. It was no good; her concentration was gone. Finally, she put the book down, got up and turned the light off, and got back into the bed. However, she almost never went to sleep, and the sleep she got was fitful and tiring.

The next morning when Corina got up and checked on momma, she found that momma had died sometime during the night. She had only seen one other dead person, and that was several years before. Momma's skin was cold; it had a whitish glare to it. Her eyes were closed. Her face looked at peace. Her body was rigid and fixed. Corina just knew that momma was dead.

"Where are you, Brad?" she asked out loud. "What do I do now?"

There was a knock on the door, and Miss Brenda called out, "Is anybody up in there?"

"Come in. Come in. Oh, please come in."

"What's wrong?" Brenda Perkins asked.

"Momma's dead. I woke up this morning and found her." Corina began to cry.

"You poor thing. I am so sorry. Does anybody else know?"

At that time they heard the noise of Doctor Fraley's old pickup out in the front yard.

"That sounds like the doctor; I'm sure glad he's here. He'll know what to do now."

Corina and Brenda Perkins both hurried out the door and met the doctor before he could even get out of his truck. They both huffed and puffed beside the truck door. The sun was already climbing up in the sky, but the morning air was still cool. Dr. Fraley could tell something was wrong.

"What's the matter? Your momma?" he asked.

"She's dead," Corina answered, out of breath.

"Let's go see," the old man replied, getting out of the truck.

Corina led the way, the doctor behind her, and Miss Brenda behind him. They all stood beside momma's bed. The doctor could tell momma was dead the second he saw her. At first nobody said a word. Dr. Fraley put his arm around Corina, and she started to cry.

"I was afraid of this. I wasn't sure she would make it through the night, but there was not a thing we could do for her. If I was right, she needed a kidney transplant." He took the end of the covers and pulled them up over momma's face.

"What will we do now? What will I tell Brad?"

"Brad will understand, and he will be so helpful," Miss Brenda reassured Corina.

"I will call the funeral home and take care of all the arrangements," Dr. Fraley said.

"Thank you. I don't know anything about all that," said Corina.

Then they heard another car stop outside the cabin.

"Who can that be?" Corina asked.

"Perhaps it's Brad," Miss Brenda said.

"That would be just wonderful."

Corina and Brenda Perkins both walked over to the front door. Corina opened the door and looked outside. A smile of relief lit up her face as she watched Brad get out of the old Chevrolet. He dropped his duffle bag on the front lawn and thanked the man inside the car. He turned around and faced the cabin. His left hand and lower arm were still in a cast. He used a cane to walk with. His green beret fit perfectly on his head. His dress uniform was full of medals. He wore the Congressional Medal of Honor around his neck. Even though he walked with a limp, there was pride and honor in his steps. He presented the image of a perfect billboard soldier.

Corina ran out the door and quickly embraced her brother. She was crying fitfully. Brad held her and let her cry for a few minutes.

"Oh, Brad, I'm so glad you're home," Corina said.

"Nothing could be so terrible," Brad replied. "I'm home now."

"Momma died last night. I found her this morning." Corina quickly told Brad about the doctor's visit and his plans to take momma to a Birmingham hospital.

Brad pulled Corina away and looked into her tear-stained face. He was shaking his head. "Momma's not dead. You're just kidding, and it's not really very funny."

Brad had not seen the doctor's truck parked over to the side under one of the trees. The doctor stood in the doorway and walked out to where Brad and Corina were. When Brad saw Dr. Fraley, a sense of shock came over him. "Dr. Fraley, is momma dead? Is that why you are here?"

"Yes, I'm sorry to say but she passed during the night."

"What? Why? How?" demanded Brad.

"Come inside and I'll explain," the doctor offered.

Then Brad saw Brenda Perkins standing in the door. "Who is she?"

Corina introduced them and told Brad quickly about Miss Perkins.

Everybody followed Dr. Fraley back into the cabin. Then Brad saw momma on the bed with the covers pulled up over her head. His knees got weak and began to tremble. He walked over to the bed, using the cane with his good arm and hand. He pulled back the covers and looked down at momma. He slumped down into the chair beside the bed and started to cry. He leaned over and kissed momma on the forehead. Nobody said a word; they all just watched Brad and momma.

Brenda walked over beside Brad and put her hand on his arm. "She was a fine lady."

"She was. She was the best lady that ever walked on the face of the earth." Brad looked up at Brenda and half smiled at her. "Thanks for being so kind to my family."

"It was nothing. You have a family to be proud of."

Again the old doctor offered to stop by the funeral home and make the arrangements. He left and assured them someone would be by soon to take the body.

Two days later Brad, Corina, Brenda, the doctor, and others attended momma's funeral.

What the preacher said at the graveside made the biggest impact.

"The greatest news that anybody can have is that a loved one in coming or going home. All of us after a long trip like to get back home. Momma had a long and happy trip here on earth. Let us who are still on our earthly trip rejoice that momma has gone home."

The Wee Pea

Folks in the valley knew farmer Ken for the productive garden he raised year after year. The climate was perfect. Just the right amount of rain fell. The sun shone at its best in this valley. Neighbors from miles around came to visit farmer Ken and his family and to admire his garden.

"Look how tall the corn is."

"Look how red the tomatoes are."

"Look how green the lettuce is."

"Look how big the watermelons are."

However, not a single human being realized there was a tiny world right there in front of them. The green peas enjoyed the valley the most. In fact, they had developed a society of their own. There was a king pea and a queen pea. All the peas loved their royalty and went out of their way to support and protect their king and queen.

In this pea society they practiced a caste system. There were the lords and the servants. There were the business peas and the farmer peas. Every pea knew his or her place. No pea would ever dare to question his station in life. Every father pea and mother pea made it a family goal to teach their heritage to their little peas.

All this went perfectly well til the O'Henrys had a wee pea. The midwife told the proud parents their son was different, special in some sort of way. She didn't understand it totally; she just knew he was different and destined for some fame or fortune. In the past this midwife had gotten in trouble for encouraging parents to educate their little peas and cause them to think, and not simply accept things as they found them.

The midwife liked to keep up with "her little peas". When wee pea was six years old, the midwife came back for a visit. Even then wee pea was full of questions:

> Why is the corn taller than the peas?
> Why are the tomatoes red and peas green?
> Why is lettuce green like peas?
> Why are watermelons larger than peas?

The midwife patiently answered every question. She even told wee pea about the great spiritual Pea in the sky. That concept was beyond wee pea's understanding. He took it to heart and thought about it often in the future.

All the neighbors tried to discourage wee pea's parents from educating wee pea and from putting all those foreign contrary ideas in his little mind. It would corrupt him, and the king and queen would not like that at all.

When wee pea was fifteen years old, two things came into his life that changed his future forever. His father bought him a green pea dictionary, and his mother got him a guitar to wile away the early evenings. Also, at this time wee pea discovered little girl green peas. This, too, caused a change in his life.

"The more words a pea knows," his father asserted, "the better off he will be."

"Yes, and if you can play the guitar and sing," his mother added, "the more the other peas will want you around."

"I think I understand," wee pea replied, "and the more words I know and the better I can play and sing, the more the girls will take a liking to me."

His mother and father grinned and shook their heads up and down.

"Just remember, son, you are special and a great future awaits you."

"Do you believe that?" wee pea asked.

"Yes, son, we do," his mother reaffirmed.

"What if I were to memorize this dictionary and to become the best guitar player and singer in this valley?"

"That would be so wonderful," his mother said.

Wee pea took the dictionary and the guitar to his room. He lay the guitar down on the bed and held the dictionary in both hands. "Then I'm going to memorize this here whole book and learn to play and sing better than any pea has ever done before."

In those days there were no schools for young peas to attend. The king and queen spread throughout the land what they wanted their subjects to know and to think. That is how so many peas grew to adulthood: being taught at a distance by the king and queen. Nobody even dared to question the system. That was just the way things were.

One day as wee pea was strolling through the valley memorizing the dictionary, he saw two girl peas picking flowers near the spring. It was a perfect day. Both peas looked as if they had jumped off a painting. They had long curly hair and bright blue eyes. Their white dresses fell down below their knees. The feeling in wee pea's heart had never been there before. He didn't understand why his heart raced so.

"Those are pretty flowers you are picking."

"Thank you. Do you like flowers?"

"Yes. I don't know many of their names. I like to look at them and to smell them."

"What's the book you are reading?" one asked, pointing to the dictionary.

"It's a dictionary. I'm not really reading it."

"What are you doing with it?"

"I'm memorizing it."

"You're what? Why are you doing that?"

"Well, I like flowers, but I like words even better."

"Isn't it hard to understand, much less memorize, the dictionary?"

That was the younger sister talking, and wee pea took a liking to her from that day on. "Would you like for me to show you a few words?" wee pea asked.

"Yes, I can't read well. You will have to help me."

"It's easy; I'll show you."

Wee pea and the younger sister walked a little way off from the older sister who was not at all interested in words or the dictionary or anything like that. The older sister returned to picking flowers and ignored the other two peas who were absorbed in the dictionary.

"Look here at this word," wee pea said.

"Which word?" sweet pea asked.

"This word is quandary, and it means to be difficult or perplex."

"What does that mean?" sweet pea asked.

Wee pea smiled and said, "Look at this word. It is indigenous and means to be a native or to be inborn. Did you know that green peas are indigenous to this valley?"

Sweet pea blushed. She didn't understand much of what he was trying to explain.

"You see, I really like words. That's why I'm going to memorize this whole book."

"How long will it take?"

"I don't know. Perhaps all my life, but that doesn't matter. It'll be worth it."

Sweet pea began to admire wee pea from that day. She didn't really want to do all that work herself, but she certainly had respect for the person who did.

"You know what else I do?" wee pea asked.

"What?"

"I play the guitar, and I sing."

"Will you play and sing for me one day?"

Wee pea felt his heart race again. "I'd like that a lot."

Wee pea and sweet pea set a date for three days later, when they would once again meet at the same spring among the beautiful flowers. Sweet pea and her sister went home with a basket full of blue and yellow and red flowers. Sweet pea went home, also, having her heart and mind longing for the next time she and wee pea would meet.

Wee pea returned home in the most joyous mood. He went right up to his room to play a song or two that he would play for sweet pea. He also learned three more words that he intended to share with sweet pea. He didn't realize how strong the influence sweet pea already had over him. He simply wanted to make a good impression.

His mother came up to his room and stood at the door. "I heard you playing. It sounded so good. Where did you go this afternoon?"

"I met a girl by the spring." He acted sort of shy and embarrassed.

"Oh, what is her name?"

"Sweet pea."

"Now, isn't that a pretty name. Do you like her?"

"Well, I just met her, but, yes, I think I do like her."

"Do you plan to see her again?"

"Yes." Wee pea told his mother about their date by the spring.

"Does she like words, too? I know she'll like your singing and playing."

"She acts like she doesn't know much about words or books.

"That is too bad. I bet you can help her."

"I bet I can, too."

The day came for the date. When wee pea saw sweet pea, she was sitting by the spring. Her face was serious and with a frown. It appeared that she had just received some bad news. Wee pea had no idea what was on her mind. He waved as he walked up to her and showed her the dictionary and his guitar.

"I've been looking forward to this time," wee pea said.

"I'm afraid I have some bad news."

"What's that?" He couldn't imagine what could be so bad.

"My parents don't want me to see you."

"Why?"

"There's talk around the village about you."

"Talk? What kind of talk?"

"Other peas are telling my parents that you are too uppity. You're trying to change what has always been done."

"I don't understand."

"Your daddy is a farmer pea; you should be a farmer pea."

"I don't want to be a farmer pea?"

"Why not?"

"Because I like words and playing my guitar."

"How will you take care of a family with words and your guitar?"

"I'm not sure. I have faith things will work out okay in my life. What do you think?"

"I think it's your life and other peas should stay out of it."

"How can I change your parents' minds?"

"I'm not sure. Right now I can only see you if I lie or sneak off."

"I don't want you to have to do that, but I do want to see you. I want to teach you all about words. I want to play and sing for you."

"Let's see how things go. I come to the spring almost daily. It wouldn't be bad if you happen to be here when I come to visit and pick flowers."

"What about your sister?"

"Oh, she met this farmer pea's son and will spend lots of time with him."

"I think we have a plan."

For a long time wee pea and sweet pea met at the spring 'by accident'.

Sometime later word came to the village that the king and queen were coming for a visit. All the peas were in an uproar readying themselves for the visit. Everybody was trying to outdo the other in preparation. Time and effort were used with abandon. The village had never been so honored.

Some of the neighbors let on to wee pea's parents that the king and queen were coming to check on wee pea. It was amazing that word of wee pee had reached even into the castle of the king and queen. Did they need to hide wee pea? Should they send him out of the valley for awhile? These were some of wee pea's parents' thoughts. They did not come to a certain conclusion. However, they were convinced nothing they had done or nothing wee pea had done was worthy of the king and queen's attention. Certainly, they had not broken any written law.

So, they decided to do nothing. Wee pea should go on living his normal life, and let the royal pair observe what was really happening in their little village. When the royal pair did arrive, the king was trying to decipher an old book written by a wise philosopher. He had trouble completely understanding the book because of the vocabulary the writer had chosen to use to get his ideas across.

The king called for the queen. "I need help understanding this book by wise pea."

The queen reached for the book. "May I look at it?"

The king handed her the book. She flipped through the pages. On page 124 she tried to read the first paragraph, but it made absolutely no sense to her. "What does this mean?" she asked.

"I don't know; that's why I need some help."

The queen asked for the king's scholars. It seemed that all the scholar peas were back at the castle working on another project for the king. The king was so upset that he could not sleep at all.

"I need help," the king admitted, "and I need it now. My mind is starting to hurt because I am straining to understand this great book. I can't sleep, and I'm starting to get irritable and fussy."

"Let me see what I can do to find something here."

"What? In this small village. What can you possibly find here?"

The word went out throughout the village that the king needed someone to help him read some book that he brought with him from the castle. Nobody bothered to tell wee pea or his parents about the king's problem. All the king's men searched the village to find the help the king so desperately needed. It was all for naught. There was no help. The king got fussier and fussier and became like a walking zombie.

One day wee pea met sweet pea at the spring. She told wee pea about the king.

"I bet I could help him," wee pea said.

"Do you really think so?"

"If I don't know the words already, I could look them up in my dictionary. I may already know the words. I could play and sing to help him go to sleep and get his rest."

"That would be great." Sweet pea wondered if wee pea really was destined to be great and famous.

That afternoon wee pea told his parents about the king and the philosophy book and his need to sleep. They suggested that he go to where the king and queen were staying and ask to speak with the king.

"What do I say?" asked wee pea.

"Just say you think you can help the king and you would like to speak with him."

"That's all?"

"That's all."

The next morning wee pea got up early and got ready to walk over to the inn where the king and queen and their court were staying. He was excited and worried. What if the king would not see him? What if he made a fool of himself? What if the king would see him, and what if he really did help the king? Perhaps even his guitar playing and singing might help the king feel better.

"What do you want?" the armed guard demanded.

"I want to see the king."

"You!" he laughed. "The king has no need of a wimpy pea like you. Get on."

"I can help the king with his problem."

Fortunately, the captain of the guard passed the station at that time and overheard their conversation. He knew how bad off the king was. "Let the boy pass."

"Yes, captain."

"I'll take him to the king myself."

The king was in the study still trying to understand the book. His eyes were red, and he needed a shave. He looked and acted tired. At this point he was past frustration. Then he heard the footsteps outside the study. "Who's out there?" he called.

"The captain of the guard and a lad."

"Go away; I'm busy."

"But, sire, this boy claims he can help you."

"Impossible. Go away."

"But, sire, it's the boy with the dictionary and the guitar."

The boy with the dictionary and the guitar. Perfect. Why hadn't the king thought of the boy with the dictionary? "Bring him in."

"Come here, lad, and speak with the king."

"What is your name?" the king asked.

"Wee pea."

"Tell me about your dictionary and guitar. I have heard a lot, and none of it is good."

Wee pea told the king about the midwife and about his parents giving him the dictionary and the guitar. He told about his desire to memorize the dictionary and to become the best guitar player and singer in the valley.

"I don't guess that's all bad," the king admitted. "Let me show you the book and see if you can explain the words to me."

"And afterwards I'd like to play and sing for you, sire."

"Yes, yes, of course."

The king handed the book to wee pea. The only book that wee pea had ever seen was the dictionary. To see the words make up sentences and paragraphs was new to him. "What are the words that bother you?"

The king showed wee pea three major words that confused him and prevented him from understanding the book. Wee pea knew two words and what they meant. He had to look up the other word. He carefully explained their meanings to the king. The king's face lit up, and he laughed out loud. There were light and life again in the king's court.

"That's it. That makes sense. I get it. Yes, the wise philosopher was so right. He wrote from personal experience."

The king sat back in his big throne-like chair and relaxed a little. Wee pee picked up his guitar and began to sing and play, softly and sweetly. Within minutes the king was fast asleep and was snoring loud enough to wake up himself. The captain of the guard found the queen and brought her to the chamber.

"Look," she whispered, "the king sleeps. That is great; he certainly needs it."

The queen escorted wee pea out of the chamber. She thanked him over and over and assured him that the king would contact him the next day. The next day the king did in fact contact wee pea. He beckoned him back to the study.

"I want you to come back to the castle with me," the king said to wee pea.

"I am honored, sire, but what can I do?"

"I want you to be one of my scholars."

Wee pea didn't know what to say.

"And I want you to become the official court musician."

"Am I that good?"

"You put me to sleep, didn't you?"

"Yes, sire, that I did."

At home wee pea explained to his parents what the king said. They were excited, but all along they expected something special to happen to their son. However, in their minds the thought of him ending up living with the king and queen in the castle never occurred. In fact, the whole village was honored to have one of their own in the castle.

After wee pea had served in the king's court for a year or so, he told the king about his relationship with sweet pea. The king invited sweet pea and her parents to come live in the castle. Six months later wee pea's parents moved to the castle.

Wee pea continued to memorize the dictionary and to play the guitar and sing. He and sweet pea were married and had several little peas. The king and queen were proud of their growing family. Wee pea and sweet pea's parents become the best of friends. In all of pea land none were better known than the king's scholar and official musician.

Year after year folk continued to visit farmer Ken and admire his garden. The valley was the talk of the land. However, not a single human being was aware of the pea kingdom right there in farmer Ken's garden.

The Ride of a Lifetime

I suppose most folk don't believe in aliens and space ships. Neither did I; at least not until about three months ago. That is when I took the ride of my life. It all happened like this:

I live in Jasper, Alabama. Ours is a small town northwest of Birmingham. Not a lot happens in our town. I used to go to work, go home, watch TV, go to bed, go to work, go home, etc, etc. I am married with two grown kids. My wife and I are still in love. However, my life is not really exciting. In fact, my kids used to always, and still do, say to me, "dad, you and mom need to get a life." I couldn't even relate to what they were saying; I was so set in our lifestyle.

My name is Tony McKnight. I am fifty-three years old. I am already bald. My head sparkles in the sunlight. I played football in high school but was not very good. I ran a little track. I tried out for basketball all my years in high school, but I was the first one cut each year. I like to dance, but my wife and I have not been to a dance in years. I am ten pounds overweight. I have never been much of a church person; although, I am a believer.

I used to be a salesman but got tired of the rejection and the unsteady income. I got a job as a night watchman at a nearby factory. I got hired because I would work the various schedules.

One night I left the house about 1:30 AM. Except for Highway 78 all the streets were silent and dark. When I pulled out of my drive, I thought I saw a shooting star above me. It was an eerie bluish-green light that flickered and zigzagged. It climbed over and dove under the clouds. It seemed like a drunk was at the steering wheel. I giggled and looked for a heavenly policeman to arrest that ole shooting star.

Then I noticed a bright light shining on the star from the earth below. It was as a spotlight dancing with a singer on a stage or like a search light from a nearby airport looking for a lost plane. Suddenly the star fell toward earth, and I lost sight of it in some nearby trees.

I thought that my eyes were just playing tricks on me and that I didn't really see what I just saw. I turned off Highway 78 and headed north toward the factory. About a mile and a half from the factory I saw ahead of me on the side of the road what looked like a young lady with a hood over her head and wearing a long black coat. She took a step like she was going to cross the road in front of me. I hit the brakes. That lady melted into a liquid and flowed across the road and then turned back into a lady.

I knew I was sick and was undergoing a psychotic breakdown. I decided if I was going crazy, I might as well enjoy it. The lady was still standing by the road. I eased up beside her. It wasn't a her; it had the face of a pig.

"Is this the planet Treniflo?" it asked. The lips didn't move as it talked.

"No, this is the planet earth."

"Oh, computers, I missed again."

"You missed. What's Treniflo?" I was having fun, nuts or not.

"It's what is called in some languages home. My preceptors are expecting me at the medium time. As usual I am lost."

"What are preceptors?"

"What some languages call parents. I don't really have time to teach you what words we use on Treniflo."

"Fine," I said. "How can I help you?"

"Do you have any spare energy I can borrow? I will repay you within this whole century."

"Within this century," I laughed. "You can repay my descendants. What kind of energy do you need?"

"Oh, computers, you don't know what energy is? There's one kind of energy." It sounded like it was using sarcasm with me.

"Do you need electricity? Are you out of gas?" I asked.

"Don't be so antiquated with me?"

"Listen, fellow. Don't pay any attention to me. I am plum crazy, and now I'm just along for the ride."

There was a renewed interest in the thing's voice. "Do you really want to go for a ride?"

"A ride? Where?"

"To Treniflo, of course."

"I got nothing to lose; let's go."

That pig-headed thing melted again to a liquid and flowed toward the trees. I didn't know what to do, so I just stood there. That thing flowed back to me, and something like an arm and hand come up and pulled me toward the trees. The hand had a ring on the ring finger shaped like a computer. By this time I was begging to wake up out of this nightmare. If I were drunk, I wanted to be sober. If I were sick, I wanted to be healed. If I were crazy, again I decided it really didn't matter. I went along for the ride of my demented life.

It pulled me past several trees and into a bushy area. Then in the moonlight I saw what looked like a giant two-story coffee cup. All it needed was a refill and some cream and sugar. It flowed up to the base of the coffee cup and changed again into a semi-human form.

"Let me open the door, and we'll go in."

"What is this?"

"This is what you would call my car."

"I see, and we're going to take a ride?"

"You bet your bottom's up."

"What does that mean?"

"I was trying to mimic your language."

"I think you confused two sayings."

"Oh, computers. I scanned your nearby library and tried to refresh my memory cells concerning your English language."

"You learn quickly."

"Of course, I am from the planet Treniflo."

"Where exactly is this planet Treniflo?"

"I am going to show you."

"You mean that's where we're taking a ride to?"

"Right on, cowboy."

It opened the door, and we entered the coffee cup. There was only one floor. Tubes ran all over the place, on the floor, up the walls, through the air. I never saw anything like that before. I must have looked surprised.

"Looks strange to you?" It said.

"Indeed it does." At this point I knew that I had flipped my lid and there was no possible help that would revive me.

"On Treniflo we mostly exist in our liquid form. We travel and communicate in these tubes. Actually, in our solid state and in our gas state we have very little power. That is why I am always in a hurry to return to my liquid state."

"Before we take off or before you crank up this coffee cup, what do I call you?"

"You mean what is my name?"

"Yes, what is your name?"

"My name is Nossel."

"Nossel?"

"Yes, and that is how you say it."

"Nice to meet you; my name is Tony McKnight."

"As you say: nice to meet you."

"The pleasure is all mine."

"Tony, if you'll excuse me, I am almost empty of energy and must feed myself."

"Sure, go ahead; I ate before I left my house."

"If you want, there is what you call an old-fashioned TV on the wall that you can watch while I replenish my energy."

Nossel went to what looked like a bathtub and melted into his liquid state. He filled the bathtub. In a few minutes gunky white stuff began to drop into the bathtub. I suppose it was what Nossel was to eat and replenish his energy. TV was available to me anytime. I had never seen an alien eat. I decided to bypass the TV and instead watch Nossel.

The white gunk disappeared as soon as it fell into Nossel's liquid form. After a few minutes I heard what sounded like a belch come from the bathtub. Later I heard what sounded like someone passing gas. Several bubbles floated to the service and popped. The rankest odor I ever smelt followed. The odor lasted a few seconds only, fortunately.

"I guess even aliens have to let it rip now and then," I laughed out loud.

It took Nossel about twenty minutes to replenish his energy supply. Later when he returned to his solid state, he looked refreshed and good as new.

"Are you ready for that ride?" Nossel asked.

"Ready," I replied.

"Let me explain something: I and this whole ship are going to turn to our liquid state in order to travel faster. We have a long way to go, and we have so little time."

"What about me?" I asked.

"Oh, you have to go to your liquid state, too."

"What?" I almost screamed.

"Oh, computers, you mere earthlings are such weaklings. It won't hurt; in fact you will enjoy the experience."

"Man, I'm already nuts as a fruit cake. I have absolutely nothing to lose."

"Good. So stand in that big bowl over there." He pointed as he spoke.

I went and got in the bowl."

"Tony. When we get back, it may take me a few tries to get you back exactly as you are now in your solid state."

"What are you saying?" I was ready to go back to MY car.

"I am expert in turning me into a solid, but I am just now getting the hang of turning others into their solid state."

"Have you ever killed anyone or done away with them?"

"No, on Treniflo we don't die."

"You live forever?"

"In a way, yes. After a long passage of time we lose our ability to turn to our gas and solid states."

"What happens then?"

"We flow into an eternal ocean and live on forever."

"How poetic."

"Sit down in the bowl and get ready for takeoff."

Nossel got back into his bowl. I sat down. The coffee cup started to rumble. I looked around, and I began to melt into my liquid state. It didn't hurt; in fact it tickled a little bit. I filled my bowl and felt like I was swimming under water or was suspended in water. I didn't feel anything. I tried to speak, but I had no mouth to talk with. I couldn't hear; I had no ears. I couldn't move; I just juked around in the bowl as apparently we flew threw the air far out into space. Only if I knew where Treniflo was.

I noticed what seemed like a sound way off in the distance. I couldn't make out what it was. Gradually the sound grew louder and louder. Finally it sounded like a voice. It was calling, "Tony! Tony!"

I realized the sound of the voice was coming from deep inside me. I tried to answer but couldn't speak. I tried again and then gave up. As I gave up and got over the anxiety and became relaxed, something inside me by my will power thought, "What? Who is it? What do you want?"

Back came the answer, "Tony, it's me Nossel. You are a quick learner. In your liquid state you can only communicate through your thoughts."

"I think I understand, but it sure seems strange. Are you sure this is real, or am I just closer to going over to the complete crazy side?"

"Oh, computers, Tony. You humans are so, so, so simplistic. Yes, that's the word, simplistic."

"Is there a difference between being simplistic and being nutty?"

"You mean like a fruit cake?"

"Exactly. Am I really here, and am I really in 'my' liquid state?"

"Yes, sir ree bob. You really are here, and we are getting mighty close to my planet Treniflo."

"What happens next?" I was getting pretty good at this think-communicate.

"Why, we get out and take a look around. I have to get you back in time to get to work on time, and I have to get this here vehicle back to my preceptors soon."

"How close are we?"

"We just passed Blexicalip where my old friend Hackel lives. We will be landing on Treniflo in about three nicomiatats."

I had no idea what one nicomiatat was, let alone three. I supposed we were so close it really didn't matter if I knew or not.

"Again, Tony, let me advise you that I often have some trouble turning others to their solid state. I'll try not to hurt you and make this as quick as possible."

I want to go home, I thought. Nossel heard me and said, "You will be home in a short time. Have a little faith in me."

That's just what I have, a little faith in you, I thought. If I were a betting man I would bet Nossel laughed and smiled when he heard that thought of mine. Without the least amount of motion the coffee cup shut down, and I realized we were on Treniflo.

I felt nothing; I saw nothing; I heard nothing; I touched nothing; I smelt nothing. It was like I was simply suspended in time and space and was almost non-existent. In my thoughts I longed to return to my solid state and to my prior life; that was life to me. If Nossel failed, what would I do? What could I do? Would I be a liquid the 'rest of my life?' I sure hoped not.

"Think positively." I heard Nossel say deep in my thoughts.

"I'm trying. I'm trying."

I don't know if Nossel had to experiment in bringing me back from my liquid state or if he was successful the first time. It didn't really matter to me. At some point I realized I was standing in my bowl (me, in my solid state).

"There you are," Nossel said.

"Thanks. I was worried."

"Oh, computers, and oh, ye of little faith," he said.

"Are we on Treniflo?" I asked.

"Yes, sir ree bob. This is home sweet home."

"Do I get to see?"

"Of course. Follow me."

Somehow Nossel opened the door, and we gazed out on what looked like a large aquarium without any fish swimming around. It was weird. There were tubes running all over the place, and those tubes were open at the top. We could look over and down and see what looked like murky water flowing through most of the tubes.

"Look, there goes Myreef Ghotley. He thinks he owns all of Treniflo. And there goes Shereet Becloft. She is the prettiest thing on Treniflo. Do you see what I'm pointing at and talking about?"

"Yes." I shook my head in amazement. "However, it all looks like just a bunch of liquid flowing through the tubes. I can't make out anything."

"Your senses are not trained, and you have not experienced your liquid state enough."

"Oh, yes I have," I reassured Nossel.

"Oh, no!" he said.

"What's the matter?" I asked.

"There go my preceptors. We have to leave now. If they pick up my wave particles, I am, as you say on earth, doomed."

"What would they do?"

"I shudder to even imagine."

"Then we need to return to earth?" I needed a yes answer. I still was convinced that I was so crazy I was beyond both treatment and hope.

"Yes, we must leave immediately."

"Let's go; I'm ready."

I must have had a questioning look on my face because Nossel asked, "What's the problem?"

"Can I ask you a question?"

"Oh, computers, sure you can."

"Is this all real, or am I only dreaming, or totally nuts?" Now if I were dreaming or was nuts, what was Nossel supposed to say to me.

"No, sir ree bob, this is all real."

"How can I prove it to myself or to others after I get back to earth?"

"There is an element in beings from Treniflo that has not been discovered yet on earth. There are traces of it deep in the earth's crust. I noticed it when I first scanned earth."

"What is it called?"

"It is called lagiostipetite. That will prove the reality of your story and of your trip to Treniflo."

"Where am I going to get this, this, what did you call it?"

"Lagiostipetite."

"Well, where do I get it?"

"Oh, computers. From me, of course," Nossel replied.

"Of course."

"This is what we are going to do."

I thought to myself: this had better be pretty good. I don't see one person on earth believing I took a ride in a coffee cup to outer space, let alone to Treniflo.

"When we get back to earth, I will turn you into your solid state before I do myself. You take that container over there next to your bowl and dip out of my bowl enough to almost fill the container."

"Then what?" I asked.

"Oh, computers, you humans worry far too much. Let me take care of the details."

"That's fine with me."

I got into my bowl, and Nossel turned me into my liquid state. The experience was not as rough as the first time. That is really about all I remember about the trip back from Treniflo to earth. The next thing I recall is our being on earth and me being in my solid state. I did as Nossel told me; I took the container and dipped out of Nossel's liquid form without spilling any.

Deep in my mind I heard someone saying, 'you take care of yourself,' and 'perhaps we will meet again sometime in the future.' I knew it was Nossel communicating to me from his liquid state. I tried hard to tell him thanks and that I wished him the best.

Without realizing the change I found myself inside my car parked in front of the factory where I worked. At that moment I knew I had been dreaming or that I was completely crazy. That is until I noticed a box in the seat beside me. I picked it up and opened it. Inside was a hand, but not an ordinary hand. It had a ring on the ring finger that was the shape of a computer. All that I had experienced was real, and Nossel had given of himself so that I could prove I took the ride of a lifetime.

"Thanks, Nossel," I said, and I went to work.

In my mind I can still hear Nossel say, "Oh, computers."

Act Like You Don't Know Me

"How much is that cotton candy there at the end of the row?"

"I don't see a price on it."

"Sixty-five cents," the man at the counter said.

The girl was probably nineteen years old. She had red hair tied back in a pony tail. She wore blue jeans with a hole in both knees. She was bare footed and had a cigarette stub hanging out one corner of her mouth. She had a moon tattooed on her neck. She did not smile, and the expression on her face said she was exhausted and frustrated.

The man she asked about the cotton candy had come to the Texaco station for a late night snack. He got a Coke and some peanuts. Before he left, he saw the girl interact with two young men who came into the store.

"Hey, Rose," one said.

"Long time no see," the other said.

Rose recognized them both instantly. She looked quickly at the car out at the gas pump. She looked back at the two. "Quiet," she said. "Act like you don't know me."

"What's the matter, baby?"

"My husband's outside getting gas."

"Your husband?"

"Yes, my husband."

Both men had shaved heads and eye brows. They were muscular and looked as if they lifted weights. Each wore a leather vest. One had a wad of cold chewing tobacco in his mouth. The other carried a bottle of beer. Both had tattoos of a Harley motor cycle on their left upper arms. Both wore black leather boots that zipped up on the sides. Their stride and expressions revealed clearly they were out for a night of excitement.

"Why'd you go and get married?"

"Cause I have a little baby."

"That's what you get for crawling in the bed with every Tom, Dick, and Harry."

"I bet you miss that, too, don't you?" Rose asked.

"Yea, you were good for a round or two."

"You got five dollars I can borrow?" Rose asked.

"For what?"

"For milk for my baby."

"For your baby!" one mimicked her.

"Yes, she is hungry. Please."

"Say pretty please with sugar on top."

"Pretty please with sugar on top."

"Get the milk, and I'll pay for it."

Rose looked out the window. "No, please, give it to me. He must not see us together."

"Is your old man jealous?"

"Yes, very much."

"You married to a man's man, I see."

"Just give me the five dollars, please."

He gave her a five dollar bill and told her to keep the change. Rose got a bottle of milk, a bag of cotton candy, and a pack of chewing gum. She paid for them and returned to the car where her husband was putting the nozzle back on the pump.

"What'd you get?" he asked.

"A bottle of milk, a bag of cotton candy, and a pack of chewing gum."

"What did you get for you?"

"Nothing," Rose answered. "I really don't want anything."

"Well, thanks for getting me the gum and cotton candy."

Rose's husband went in the Texaco station and paid the man three dollars for the gas. The two other men stared at him. He felt uneasy but didn't say anything. He returned to the car and got in. He had dark black hair that needed washing and combing. He had his overalls on from work. Most of his lower teeth were rotted out, and he had sour breath that reeked from five feet away. He dropped out of school in the ninth grade and went to work to support his mother and three brothers after their father deserted them.

It took four tries to get the car started. The front right side was dented from where he had run off the road and hit a tree. Springs popped through the back seat. There was no back seatbelt to hold the baby carrier in place. There were an empty beer can and a Baby Ruth wrapper in the back floorboard.

"Jesse, I'm glad we got married after I had Carolyn."

"Do you know those two motorcycle guys in the store?" Jesse asked.

"No, why do you ask?" Rose reached back and held the baby carrier steady.

"Because I saw you being so friendly with them. What did that one give you?"

"Five dollars."

"Five dollars! What for?"

"For the milk and the cotton candy and the gum. Now I still have the three dollars you gave me to get us something to eat tomorrow."

"You know Jesse Underwood don't take no charity, don't you?"

"You told me enough times."

"How do you know those two guys?"

"That's a long story, and you don't really want to know."

"You use to ride with them?"

"Yes."

"You been in the bed with both of them?"

"Jesse, please."

"Please nothing. Have you?"

"Yes! Now you satisfied?"

"Naw. I'm sick over it."

"It was a long time ago, before I met you."

Jesse looked back at the baby in the back seat. "Let me ask you something."

"What?"

"Is Carolyn my baby?"

"Yes, Jesse. I promise she is. We've been over this many times."

"Yes, I know, but is she really?"

"Yes, Jesse, I promise you she is."

Back at the Texaco station the two men came outside and stood by their bikes and talked. They looked at each other and at their bikes. They bragged and bragged about a race they'd been in a couple of weeks back. One of them wiped the seat off and checked the oil. One looked at his watch.

"What time is it?" the other asked.

"Nine-thirty."

"Too early to go back."

"Let's go have a little fun."

"Like what?"

"Let's go get Rose and take her for a ride."

"You mean both kinds of a ride."

"I sure do!"

"Let's go."

After Jesse and Rose left the Texaco station, Jesse decided he wanted to stop and get a drink on the way home. He knew it would make Rose mad, but he was determined to stop anyway. He felt after a long day at work he deserved it. There was only one place in the world left that would give him drinks on credit.

Some two miles down the road from the gas station the car started missing and almost died. Jesse got out, opened the hood, jiggled a few wires, and got back in the car. It ran fine thereafter. Carolyn started to cry.

"She's hungry," Rose said.

"We'll stop on the way home, and you can feed her."

"Why don't we just go home?"

Jesse turned off the highway onto a gravel road. Rose knew then exactly where Jesse was going.

"We're not going to Sherry's, are we?"

"I just want one drink. It's been a long hard day. I deserve it."

"I need to feed Carolyn."

"We'll only be here about thirty minutes. That's long enough for you to feed her."

Jesse drove the car into Sherry's parking lot. It was a western low cost bar and grill where everybody knew everybody. There were ten cars and six pickup trucks parked outside. A group of cowboys were drinking beside one of the pickups. A woman and a man were dancing on the bed of the truck. One drunk slept on the far side of the truck.

Everybody waved at Rose and Jesse as they drove past and parked at the far end of the lot. Rose saw the horses and heard the cows mooing in the pasture beside them. Out behind the bar two fellows had started a fire and were roasting marsh mellows. Above the moon was full, and its light danced off the floating clouds.

The bar had been an old barn before Sherry bought it and totally redecorated it. Folks often wondered where she got the money to finance the work. It didn't matter any how because Sherry was getting rich off her investment.

Jesse got out of the car and headed for the front entrance. Rose got out and pushed her seat forward so she could get Carolyn out. Rose carried the baby, her diaper bag, and the bag from the gas station. She felt so angry when Jesse left her behind to take care of Carolyn by herself.

Jesse did open the door for Rose and Carolyn. Cigarette smoke filled the room, and the room reeked of cheap beer. Two men played chess at one of the front tables. A woman played solitaire two tables over.

In the back on a tiny stage an elderly black woman sang Hank William Sr.'s songs.

"Find us a table, and I'll get a couple of drinks," Jesse said.

"No problem. There's plenty of tables," Rose replied.

"What a cute baby," the lady playing solitaire said.

"Thanks," Rose replied.

"What's its name?"

"HER name is Carolyn. She's ten months old."

"Well, she's just the most precious thing I ever saw."

Rose sat down at a table by the window. She opened the diaper bag and took out a bottle. She took the milk out of the brown bag and filled the bottle. She cradled Carolyn in her left arm and fed her with her right hand. Carolyn sucked vigorously. Jesse started over to the table with two drinks.

The front door opened and in came three men. The leader wore a dingy white shirt and a soiled tie. The other two fellows looked like actors in a second rate movie. By this time it was difficult to see all the way across the room because of the cigarette smoke. Most of the customers knew the three and spoke respectfully to them.

"Howdy, Mr. Gunter. How ya doing?"

"Just fine, son. Just fine."

"It's good to see you, Mr. Gunter. Long time no see."

"Been busy, Joe. You know business demands so much time."

"Yes, sir. It sure does."

Jesse couldn't see Mr. Gunter, but he heard his name. He set one drink on the first table he passed and headed over to where Rose was feeding Carolyn.

"Get up and go to the bathroom, now!" he ordered Rose.

"Why? What's wrong?"

"Just do as I say. Act like you don't know me."

"What? Are you crazy; you're my husband."

"Now!" Jesse shoved Rose and Carolyn toward the bathrooms.

Jesse sat down and tried to act calm. He had an idea of what was about to take place. He patted his feet on the floor nervously. He gritted his teeth. He frowned. He picked a tiny sore on his forearm, and it bled slightly. His stomach was upset. He swallowed his drink in one gulp.

Mr. Gunter looked over the room of customers. "Looking for somebody special" a man asked.

"Yep, and I bet I find him."

"Pete!" Mr. Gunter yelled above the crowd.

"Over here, Mr. Gunter."

Pete played the piano for the lady singer. He was about sixty with white hair that hung down over his forehead and ears. His left little finger was missing, which caused him to learn to play the piano as a child after a bet that he could never learn. He had played for awhile in Las Vegas but was run out of town for failing to pay his debts.

Mr. Gunter made his way back to the stage and Pete. "Where is he?"

Pete pointed to where Jesse sat. "There. He sent his wife and baby to the bathroom."

"Wife and baby? Most interesting."

"Mr. Gunter, I got nothing against Jesse and his family. Can I stay out of this?"

"Sure, Pete. Here's twenty dollars. Thanks for the tip."

"Anytime, Mr. Gunter."

Mr. Gunter stopped at the bar and picked up a drink. He then walked over to the table where Jesse sat. Jesse saw him coming and almost fainted. The two body guards followed Mr. Gunter like little puppy dogs. Mr. Gunter motioned with his head towards the bathroom and sent one goon after Rose and Carolyn. He motioned the other goon behind Jesse. He pulled out a chair and sat down facing Jesse.

"Jesse, Jesse, my man. How have you been?"

"Not too good, Mr. Gunter. Barely making ends meet."

"That's not my problem, Jesse. My problem is five hundred dollars you owe me."

"I know, Mr. Gunter. I'll pay you. I promise."

"That's what you said two weeks ago."

"Mr. Gunter, I get paid Friday. I can pay you then."

Mr. Gunter took out a cigarette and lit it. He blew smoke in Jesse's face. Jesse looked at him through fearful eyes. The goon forced Rose to come out of the bathroom. One woman called him a pervert for entering the women's room. He laughed and smiled at her. He carried the baby and herded Rose in front of him. She carried the diaper bag. She left the milk, the cotton candy, and the gum in the bathroom.

Mr. Gunter took the baby and caressed her head. "You're a pretty little thing."

"Leave her alone," Rose demanded.

"Be quiet," Jesse said.

"Drop dead," Rose replied.

"Like the man said, shut up, lady," the goon said.

Rose slapped the goon. He started to hit her back. Mr. Gunter stopped him.

Then the front door opened, and the two males from the Texaco gas station entered the bar and grill. Right away everybody knew they were motorcycle riders. Nobody wanted trouble with them. All too often cowboys and bikers don't mix.

"Look for Rose," Hector said to Roberto.

"I can't see much for the smoke."

"These cowboys sure like to smoke."

"Let's go ask the bartender."

Hector and Roberto got their drinks and chatted with the bartender. He motioned over to the table where Rose, Carolyn, Jesse, Mr. Gunter, and the two goons were. Through the smoke they could tell something was going on at the table. They asked the bartender if he knew the three men. Of course, he did.

"Let's go see what's up," Roberto said.

Rose saw them coming toward the table. She slapped the goon by her again. He jerked his head back in reaction and started to slap Rose. Hector saw him raise his hand and raced over to the table. He grabbed his hand and twisted it up behind his back. The other goon tried to stop him, but Roberto kicked him in the leg, and he fell to the floor. That's when Mr. Gunter pulled a pistol from a holster strapped to his ankle under his pants leg. He fired one shot into the floor beside Hector's right foot.

Hector and Roberto stood still and turned their heads to look at Mr. Gunter. "Why did you go and do that?" Roberto asked.

"I didn't see your invitation to this party," Mr. Gunter said.

"Rose is our invitation. You best not hurt her."

"If I do, just what will you two monkeys do?"

"Break your neck," they said in unison.

Mr. Gunter pointed the pistol at Hector and fired. The bullet nicked him on the upper arm, and blood ran down his arm. However, he didn't flinch or blink. "Take the baby," Mr. Gunter told the two goons.

"No," Rose screamed. "What is this all about?" she asked Jesse.

"It's about money, five hundred dollars."

"What, you owe them five hundred dollars?"

"Yes."

"And you're going to just stand there and let them take your daughter?"

"What do you expect me to do? He's got a gun."

"I expect you to act like a man."

"A man doesn't have to act stupid. We'll get the baby back."

"That's the damn truth," Hector assured her.

Roberto said, "I strongly advise you to leave that baby with her mother."

"What are you going to do? Ride your putt-putt after me?"

"You'll be surprised. I'm just warning you."

Mr. Gunter took Carolyn and the diaper bag and gave them to one of the goons. "Now let's get out of here." He turned to Jesse and slapped him. "Five hundred dollars by morning."

"Yes, Mr. Gunter," Jesse answered.

"You're a real man's man," Rose blurted out at Jesse.

Mr. Gunter looked around at the customers like he dared any of them to tell what went on at the bar and grill that night. They all shook their heads as if what happened was just as normal as the black lady singing in the back on the tiny stage. Mr. Gunter threw a kiss to the singer who did not miss a single note during the entire incident. Mr. Gunter, with his two body guards and Carolyn, left the bar and grill.

After the door closed, Roberto pointed toward the bathroom and said to Hector, "Go and clean up that scratch." He then nodded toward the phone on the wall. "I'll get the boys." He turned to Rose and said, "We'll have that baby back before that butthead is back to the highway."

Before Rose could reply, Roberto was dialing the phone. "We'll meet you at the second curve before the highway."

Hector returned from the bathroom with some toilet paper stuck to his upper arm. "Just where will we meet the boys?"

"The second curve this side of the highway."

"That'll be perfect. I bet he messes in his pants when he sees what'll be waiting for him."

"Follow us in your car," Roberto told Jesse.

Hector and Roberto started up their Harleys. Jesse cranked up his car, and Rose got in the front seat beside him. Jesse and Rose followed Hector and Roberto down the road.

"I don't know what's going to happen, but I think it's not good for ole man Gunter."

"I hope they stomp them into the ground," Rose said.

Rose pointed up to the bikes. Roberto and Hector had turned their lights off. Jesse took the hint and also turned off his head lights.

"We're coming up to the curve. I hope they see Gunter's car in front of them."

They were all in the curve and the only light or sign of life was that of Mr. Gunter's car up ahead. Evidently they didn't see the bikes and the car behind them. They sure did not see what was ahead of them.

As the curve almost straightened out, Roberto and Hector turned on their lights. Behind them Jesse did the same. Mr. Gunter swerved his car slightly to the left because of the glare of the lights in his rearview mirror. Ahead of Mr. Gunter scattered all the way from one side of the road to the other in haphazard rows fifty-one bikers turned on the lights of their Harleys.

Mr. Gunter slammed on the car brakes and skidded off the road on the shoulder. Hector and Roberto raced up to the car, stood their bikes up, and banged on the car windows. Nobody got out of the car.

"Get out of the car, you morons. The fun is about to begin."

"Throw the pistol out the window first."

Mr. Gunter threw the pistol out on the ground. Hector picked it up and shot all four tires and the radiator. The car quit running.

"Out, NOW!"

Roberto shouted ahead to the other bikers, "Let's make them run the line."

"Ooh yea," one of the bikers agreed. "We haven't had that kind of fun in a long time."

"Come get the baby," Hector said to Rose.

Rose ran up to the car, got in the back seat, and gently took Carolyn out. "Thanks," she said as she passed Hector and Roberto.

"Take your shirts off," Roberto said to the three who got out of the car. He turned to the other bikers and shouted, "Alright, you guys get your belts ready. These fools need a real lesson in how they should treat my friends and their babies." Roberto turned to Rose and said, "Come here again. I think you need a little of this fun."

Rose didn't really understand what he meant. In fact, she was frightened. She carefully handed Carolyn to Jesse and eased up to Roberto and the others.

Roberto pointed to the goon who took Carolyn and slapped Rose. "Hit him."

"What?"

"Slap him again."

"Really?"

"Just do it."

Rose smiled and pranced up to the character and slapped him as hard as she could.

"Felt good, didn't it?" Roberto asked.

"It sure did." Rose grinned.

"Slap him again. Only this time even harder."

Rose drew back and bounced off one foot and hit the fellow with her fist across the mouth. He jerked back naturally and threw up his fist to hit Rose back. Hector came from behind and kicked him in the kidney. He fell to the ground in pain.

Rose went back and took Carolyn from Jesse. She looked into his face with disgust.

Roberto took Rose and Jesse aside. "You folks can leave now. It is time for us to give these morons a lesson in manners."

"Thanks," Jesse said.

"Yea, like she said: you're a real 'man's man' alright."

"Really, thanks. I don't know what we would have done if you hadn't come along," Rose said.

Roberto placed his hand on Hector's shoulder and said, "Don't ever tell us again to act like we don't know you."

Hector laughed and looked up and down Rose's body. "Baby, we're still gonna take you for a ride."

The Master

The resentful locksmith lingered cautiously while the lightning sparkled peacefully and supernaturally. The lightning danced across the evening sky dropping shadows here and there in the living room of the two hundred year old mansion. Footsteps creaked across the attic floor above. Rain tapped against the window on the other side of the room. The soft breath of the wind caused the candle light to flicker. A musty smell saturated all the furniture.

Blood dripped from the portrait of General Harold B. Blightson. Tears flowed down the face of his dear wife in the portrait beside him. Their five children hung in the paintings below them. At least, they were supposed to. However, the portrait of their youngest son lay on the step, a ragged tear down the middle of his face.

"Come in," a husky voice beckoned from inside the room.

"Do you know what time it is?" demanded the locksmith.

"I damn well do. Come in; I have a job for you."

"It sure better pay well."

"Money is the least of my concerns."

"Well, it's mighty high on my list of priorities."

Don Charter wore a red flannel shirt and blue jeans, his red hair down to his collar, his face revealing his forty-five years. His father had been a locksmith, and that was all Don knew. On the other hand,

Rodney Headstone wore a blue flannel nightshirt, his grey hair in array, his face revealing his sixty-five years. His grandfather was General Blightson, and he was a retired army colonel.

"Mr. Charter, do you believe in curses and ghosts?"

"No, but I'm not married either."

"Mr. Charter, do you want to leave here tonight alive?"

"What's that supposed to mean; you planning on killing me?"

"No, but my grandfather or one of his soldiers might."

"Who is your grandfather?"

"I'm glad you asked. Come, let me show you something."

Colonel Headstone led Don Charter across the room into the hallway and up a stairwell. Two lanterns hung at the top of the stairs and gave more light to the area than did the lone candle. A door squeaked closed at the end of the upstairs hall. A horrid scream squalled from inside the room. Charter jumped with fright.

"Don't worry, Mr. Charter. That is only my grandfather. It happens every time he thinks of the way he lost his last battle and of the way he died."

"The way he died? If he's dead, how can he scream?"

"I already asked you if you believe in ghosts and curses, and you wanted to be funny."

"I'll stop being funny. Tell me about your grandfather. I might need to leave soon."

"Mr. Charter, I promise you before you leave here tonight, you will be a believer."

Col. Headstone stopped in front of the portraits about halfway up the stairs. First, he pointed to the picture of his grandfather. "This is General Harold B. Blightson. He died the last year of the Civil War."

"Is that?"

"Yes, that is blood. This portrait bleeds on every anniversary of the General's death. He failed to do as Robert E. Lee commanded and lost every soldier under his command, even himself. First, he was shot in the leg. As he lay on the ground, a Yankee soldier knifed him with his bayonet. He bled to death within minutes."

"He's dead. I guess he's dead. So what?"

"Nobody remembers my grandfather with fond memories. He is known as the general that led all his troops to their death. At the time, and especially, after the war, there was a cry for revenge. A curse was placed on the family. Many wished him and his family nothing but misery and evil."

"So, what happened?"

"This next picture is my grandmother, the general's wife. She was ostracized by all the women in the south. She received tons of hate mail. About a year later she managed to grieve herself to death. They are both buried outback in unmarked graves. Fortunately, the general's body was stolen by one of his brothers and a cousin when the Yankees refused to return his body. Later, the bodies of his brother and cousin were found floating in a nearby lake."

"What about the children?"

"The story gets sadder and sadder. The two eldest, a son and a daughter, both died on the day of their marriage. It was like somebody knew and planned it. They were married six years apart, but both died right after the ceremony, with no signs of foul play."

"What about the youngest."

"Sadder even." Headstone pointed to the portrait on the step but did not stoop down to pick it up. "That son went missing when he was nineteen and was never seen again. The only thing that remains of him is this portrait, and it has lain there on this step for years."

"What about the curse and ghosts?"

"Aw, Mr. Charter, that is the strangest part. Look at the signature by the artist on each of these paintings."

Charter stretched to get closer. The flickering light of the lanterns and the candle didn't give off much light. He took his glasses out of his flannel shirt pocket and put them on. "It looks like Jesse P. Wells and under each signature is the title The Master."

"That is right, my dear Mr. Charter. That is right."

"So, my dear man, why am I here?"

"There is a door upstairs that I cannot get open. I either lost the key or never had it."

"Now that is something I can fix."

"I know, Mr. Charter. I know."

Col Headstone led Don Charter on up the stairs and down the hallway. They stopped in front of the third door on the left. "This is it?"

Charter thought he heard breathing from inside the room and saw light come from under the door, but decided it was only his imagination. He pulled out a string of keys with any and every size and shape. He started to try them. Finally, one fit perfectly, and he started to open the door.

"Just a minute, Mr. Charter. I need to tell you more about Jesse P. Wells, The Master. He was a most wise and evil man. He practiced the magic arts and was once tried as a witch doctor. And he was an excellent, professional painter. He had two half brothers that nobody knew about. One was killed in the Civil War. To be exact, he was the adjutant for General Blightson. He died in that fatal military muddle."

Charter opened the door a little. "Who was the other half brother?"

Col Headstone shoved the door all the way open. "He was your grandfather, the man who got your father interested in being a locksmith, and you are the only living relative of Jesse P. Wells, the man who cursed my family." Headstone kicked Charter into the room and slammed the door.

A death chilling scream filled the hallway and pounced down the stairway. Presently, General Harold B. Blightson appeared outside the closed door in the hallway.

"Grandfather, is that really you?"

"Yes, Rodney, thanks to you, I am finally at peace."

"It wasn't that hard to find any of Wells' relatives. In fact, Don Charter is the last of the line. Too bad he never married and had children of his own."

"I'm awfully tired, Rodney. I think I'll go to my room and take a nap."

"That's okay, Grandfather. I'll not bother you."

The general returned to his bedroom. The colonel went down the stairs. He stopped by the portraits. The blood on the general's had disappeared. The tears on his wife's were dried up. The youngest son's was back on the wall, and the tear was repaired.

Colonel Headstone pulled at his ear. "Who believes in curses and ghosts?"

The Vicious Affair

It was the ideal place to start having an affair. At least that's what Mrs. Vicki Richards thought. She was irate over the way she felt her husband of three years treated her. She would later learn revenge is not always worth what it costs personally. However, at the time she failed to consider any consequences and purposefully sought the right man with whom to get involved.

The sand on the beach was warm and dry. Her feet sunk slightly as she spread her towel under the umbrella. The sun hung in the middle of the sky. The waves rippled in and out, up and down the coast. The melody of the ocean swayed Vicki emotionally. She was in search of a man. Not just any man, but the right man with whom to start an affair. If she had her wishes, she was going to destroy her husband.

Three miles away out on the wharf loading his private fishing boat was Captain Jonathan Winston, a happily married man with two young children. That day he prepared for ten Japanese tourists who wanted to go deep sea fishing. The trip was only to last two hours. He had no thoughts of having an affair. However, he had secrets of which he wished his wife to know nothing. She would soon learn of his extra-curricular activities.

"Where do we hide the stuff?"

"In the tackle area, under the ropes."

"Is it safe there?"

"Yes, of course."

The last Japanese man to board the boat handed the captain ten one hundred dollar bills. He tipped his hat and rearranged his camera which hung around his neck. The captain took the money and looked around hoping nobody saw the transaction. After he helped the man into the boat, the captain latched the gate over the gangplank. They were ready to go fishing.

Back on the beach Vicki was still scoping for the right man. She started to turn red and almost decided to leave the beach for the day. Two high school kids walked past her and kicked some sand on her towel. It made her mad.

"Watch out, you punks!" she yelled.

"Look," one lad said. "The porcelain doll really talks."

The other lad added, "We could have some fun with the doll."

"Get lost!" demanded Vicki.

"You going to make us, baby?"

"The lady may not, but I will." There stood one of the seasoned life guards.

"We were only having a little fun," they both assured the guard.

"Like the lady said, 'Get lost.'"

The school kids said nothing, but sulked and wandered away.

Vicki stood up on her towel. She took time to look over this man. He might be the one she had been seeking. He was tall, but not too tall. He didn't tower over her. He had a dark copper tan. His muscles sharply outlined his body. He had sun-bleached blonde hair. She liked what she saw. This man could produce havoc for her dear husband.

He pointed toward the water. "Have you ever ridden on a Seadoo?"

"Never."

"Well, there's always the first time. Come on. It's great fun."

"Sure, why not?"

They ran on the warm sand to the portable dock and out to where the Seadoo was tied up. The wind started to pick up, and waves were turning choppy further out to sea.

"Is this a good time?' Vicki asked.

"Sure. We'll be back in a few minutes. I'll take good care of you."

"Let's go then."

He hopped on like he was mounting a horse, and she huddled up behind him. Being so near could lead to much more, she thought. They headed out into the water away from the shoreline. Within a few minutes the winds whipped up furiously, and the waves were well over their heads. The shoreline was totally out of view.

The captain of the fishing boat, his crew, and the Japanese had already headed back to the wharf. Jonathan not only wanted to save his ship and the men on board, but he wanted to also save his precious cargo. There was no time to waste.

"How far out are we?" his Japanese comrade asked him.

"Not far. We'll be back in a few minutes. The motor on this baby is much stronger than any of these waves or wind."

On the Seadoo the ride turned disastrous. Vicki was screaming, and the manly guard was worried sick seeking the shoreline.

"Where is the land?" he demanded.

"Don't you know what to do?" Vicki begged.

"Yea, babe, head for land, but I don't see land."

"Are we going to die?"

"Cool it, babe." The life guard was about to lose his cool. Vicki's reaction made him more ill at ease. He tried to calm down. He tried to remember all he had been taught and all he had taught others. It all seemed so distant at the moment.

"Look out!" screamed Vicki.

Too late. The Seadoo and the fishing boat collided head on. The bow of the boat split the Seadoo. The life guard collapsed into the water, his head crushed and his body torn. The jolt threw Vicki clear of the boat's bow. She struggled to keep her head above water. As Vicki reached out for help, Jonathan realized they had hit something. He ran to the bow where he saw blood and heard Vicki's cries for help.

"Over here," he yelled to the crew.

"Did we damage the boat?" asked one of the crew.

"I don't think so. Let's get that woman out of the water."

Vicki lay on the boat deck unconscious. She had a bruise on her forehead. Jonathan did what most others would do; he put a blanket over her and raised her head. The crew took the boat toward the wharf. The wind and the waves did not let up until the boat was well within the harbor.

Jonathan had already radioed the coast guard, and they were on their way to pick up the body of the life guard. He decided against taking Vicki to the hospital (a decision he later much regretted). Instead he took her down to his state room. The Japanese all left the boat, including the captain's comrade after he checked the security of their cargo.

The police ruled the incident an accident, and there was no further questioning. The two officers left the boat and Jonathan and Vicki alone in the belly of the fishing boat. There Vicki's evil mind went to work. Under the blanket her bikini top was torn and her breasts hung out freely. She tried to get up, and slipped back on the sofa.

Jonathan came over to check on her. She sat up and the blanket fell to the floor.

"How can I ever thank you?" she asked.

"There's no need." The captain's heart raced up as he observed the perfectly matched firm breasts.

"Yes, there is. Come here and let me show you how I can thank you."

"No. I am a happily married man."

"Who'll ever know?"

"I will."

Vicki took off her bikini bottom. The captain sat down beside her. Vicki embraced him and started to fondle him.

An hour later they sat at a restaurant off the wharf discussing the calm sea and the golden sun above. They were making plans for the future. Vicki was to move in with Jonathan aboard the ship. His wife would never know; they assured each other. Jonathan failed to share with Vicki that he had another business in addition to fishing and tourists.

"I've never had a relationship based solely on lust and sex."

"Me, either" replied Vicki, wishing her husband could have been tied and made to watch her last two hours.

"Where do we go from here?"

"Lust and sex," Vicki leaned back and laughed. Her forehead hurt as she laughed.

"I can sure go for that."

"Tell me about your fishing business."

"How about we do more lust and sex?"

"What about fishing?" Vicki wanted to know what she was getting into.

The captain didn't want to get into what he underhandedly did with his fishing boat. So, he kept his comments very general. The next day he was to pick up a load of cargo from a ship three miles out from the wharf.

"Tomorrow I plan to take a group of German tourists out fishing. It seems these tourists really like to go deep sea fishing, and I sure like their money."

"I want to go," demanded Vicki.

"Oh, no. No women aboard a ship; it's bad luck."

"Who believes in luck?"

"I do," answered Jonathan.

"Do you remember lust and sex?" Vicki threatened.

"Oh, yea."

"Well, I want to go fishing tomorrow with you. I like to fish."

From the back room Tyler Richards, Vicki's husband, observed closely the couple as they discussed their future plans. His rage boiled inside him. At that moment he wanted to rush over and kill the man at the table with his wife. Then he contrived a scheme he thought would be the ruin of both Vicki and the other man.

Tyler waited patiently until Vicki and Jonathan left the restaurant. Once outside Vicki kissed the captain passionately and they parted, to meet again later. Tyler walked to the front of the restaurant and watched a few minutes longer. The anger was burning inside him. He found the chief waiter back by the kitchen.

"Did you see the couple in the back room with the dimmed lights?"

"No," the man replied, showing a lie all over his face.

Tyler opened his wallet and showed the waiter money. "Again, did you see the couple in the back room?"

The waiter noticed the twenties and a couple of hundreds. "Yes, I believe I did, now that I think more about it."

"Do you know the man?"

The waiter smiled and looked down at the wallet of money.

"What is his name? Where does he live? Is he married?"

Tyler left knowing Jonathan's full name, address, and the status of his family. The waiter returned to work, stuffing money into his wallet.

Angela Winston, the captain's wife, was a file clerk for a local attorney. She worked for a little over minimum wage for twenty-nine hours a week without benefits. Her boss knew the law and used it to the letter. Angela was attractive but the fact she had delivered three babies showed a little. Every once in a while one of the male clerks made a pass at her.

"Angela," her supervisor held up the phone. "It's for you."

Angela put down the stack of files she held and went to the nearest office to answer the phone. "Hello, this is Angela Winston." Angela rarely got a call at work. Even Jonathan did not call her at work.

"Angela, this is Tyler Richards. We need to talk."

"About what? Who are you?"

"About your husband and my wife. They're becoming a twosome."

Angela returned to filling records. She could not believe what the man told her over the phone. Could it be possible? Would Jonathan do that to her? She fought back the tears until her break time. Then she retired to the ladies room and locked herself in. There she wept all alone.

After work Angela went home to their house in a nice subdivision. The baby sitter sat on the living room sofa watching an afternoon talk show. Both boys were in the floor playing with their Game Boys. Angela dropped her purse by the front door and fell in a recliner across from the sofa. The baby was still taking her afternoon nap.

"Can you stay tonight? I have to go out and take care of some important business."

"I'll call my parents," the baby sitter replied.

"Good. I'll fix us all some supper."

After supper and after the children were ready for bed, Angela left specific instructions for the baby sitter. She took her cell phone, which she rarely did, and gave the number to the sitter. Then she was off for her meeting with Tyler Richards.

Tyler and Angela had agreed to meet at a motel on the outskirts of town. The motel had a small café attached to the side. They sat at a back booth and ordered two drinks. Angela was nervous, but Tyler was angry and excited.

"Are you sure your wife is having an affair with my husband?"

"My wife's mad at me because I didn't take her on a business trip to San Francisco three weeks ago. Now she wants to get even by embarrassing me."

"But why my husband?"

"Vicki was just looking for a man."

"But why my husband?"

"To be honest I thought she was going to try something. So, I hired a private eye to keep tabs on her for me." Then Tyler explained what the PI had told him about his wife's last few days' activities. He shared about the life guard and Seadoo and the captain and the fishing boat and the accident. Then he asked, "How much detail do you want to know of their physical activities?"

"Spare me the details, please. I have an imagination."

"The reason I called you and shared all this," Tyler said.

"Yes, do explain that part."

Tyler smiled, and the evil intent showed all over his face. "I want to turn the screws on my lovely wife. She deserves my anger and revenge."

Angela sat back in her chair. Gradually a contented smile warmed her face. "He could have said no. He could have avoided all this. But no; he went along." She leaned up to the table. "My new friend, anger and revenge are appropriate words."

"Wait! I have not told you everything."

"What more is there?"

"Oh, there's lots more. It's the how we get our revenge."

"I want to know everything," Angela demanded. Tyler had a book with him. Angela had not seen it because of her nervousness.

Tyler placed the book on the table. "Let me show you something."

"That looks like a history book."

"In a way it is. Actually, it's a book about treasures. I told you that your husband's last customers were Japanese."

"Yes."

"That was no accident."

"What do you mean?"

Tyler opened the book to a marked page. "Here on page 145 it talks about the Imperial Regalia of Japan."

"I've never heard of that. What is it? What does that mean?"

"Let me read you something."

Angela sat back and prepared to listen.

"The Imperial Regalia of Japan, also known as the Three Sacred Treasures, consist of the sword, Kusanagi (or possibly a replica of the original), the jewel or necklace of jewels, Yasakani no magatama, and the mirror Yata no kagami. Also known as the Three Sacred Treasures of Japan, the regalia represent the three primary virtues: valor (the sword), wisdom (the mirror), and benevolence (the jewel). These may be connected with Buddhist thought."

Angela shook her head. Her forehead wrinkled. She raised her hands. "Again, what does all that mean, and what does it have to do with our pathetic spouses?"

"Look at the pictures." Tyler pointed at the pictures. "They are Japanese treasures."

"So what?" Angela was starting to get tired and confused.

"Japanese. Your husband took Japanese tourists fishing."

"He takes tourists fishing all the time. What's so important about that?"

"They stole the treasures."

Angela sat right up. A light went on in her brain. "You mean those Japanese tourists aboard my husband's fishing boat stole these

Japanese treasures?"   She pointed to the book on the table.   "And you're telling me that these treasures are aboard my husband's boat, and they are there now?"

"That's exactly what I'm trying to tell you."

"That means my dear Jonathan is now playing and fishing with the big boys."

"That means your dear husband is party to international robbery and is now on the top ten of lots of people's lists."

"Is he in danger?"

"I talk daily with my PI. He tells me your husband is in way over his head. He'll do very well to live another week or two."

Vicki ordered another refill of her drink. She rubbed her hands in front of her. "So, what are we going to do?"

Tyler put the book away. He ordered another drink and a BLT sandwich. He massaged the back of his head and neck like he had a headache. He though a few minutes like he was carefully picking his words.

"We're going to steal them."

"We're going to steal them? You mean the Japanese treasures?"

"That's exactly what I mean."

"Then what?"

"My new friend, Angela, that's the best part."

"Tell me then."

"I'll let my PI explain it; he'll be here in a few minutes. I told him to meet us here."

Shortly, a tall Japanese man came into the café. He was dressed like the other tourists. He had a camera hanging around his neck. He wore sun glasses. He came over to the table where Tyler and Angela sat. Tyler motioned for him to sit down.

"Yahimo, this is Angela Winston. Angela, this is Yahimo Shalita. He is my PI."

Yahimo bowed his head to Angela. "Nice to meet you, ma'am." He spoke in perfect English.

"Thank you. It's nice to meet you, too."

"I was just telling Angela about the treasure," Tyler said.

Yahimo sat down. "To be honest, Mrs. Winston, your husband is into something where he has no business."

"What do you mean?" asked Angela.

"He's messing around with the Japanese underground, what you might call the Japanese Mafia. He and Mr. Tyler's wife are planning on double crossing them and getting away with the Imperial Regalia of Japan. That is really stupid on their part."

Tyler interrupted. He called for the waiter to refill their drinks and to bring the menu to Yahimo Shalita. They didn't speak while the waiter was anywhere close. The PI ordered his drink and some soup to eat.

"This is where our revenge comes in, Angela."

"How's that?" she asked.

Tyler laughed and spilled some of his drink. He wiped it up with his napkin. "My friend Mr. Shalita here is going to steal the treasure, and we're going to turn the bunch of them over to the police."

"Isn't that dangerous for us?" Angela asked.

"Not the way we have it all planned out," Yahimo Shalita reassured her.

That night Yahimo Shalita returned to his office to work out the details of their plan. It was revenge in the first degree; it was also greed. Angela returned to her children. Tyler went home after stopping for another couple of drinks. Jonathan and Vicki were together aboard his fishing boat. The life guard was in a casket awaiting his funeral and burial. The Japanese were planning on getting rich from selling the Imperial Regalia of Japan. A quirk of feminine nature brought them all together.

However, later that night Yahimo Shalita attended another private meeting. It was with the Japanese tourists who stored the treasure aboard Jonathan's boat. Mr. Shalita had not been totally honest with Tyler. He 'forgot' to tell Tyler that he worked for the Japanese underground. In fact, he was a second cousin of the 'godfather' in Tokyo. The plans all along were to use the captain and then do away with him. Now Vicki Richards entered the picture and would have to go, too.

A young sexy yellow-skinned Japanese lady served tea to the room full of men. Then she shut the door after she left. For about forty-five minutes they discussed a message from Tokyo about the stolen treasure. After the discussion the leader of the group told the others to go get some sleep, all except Yahimo Shalita. They needed to decide what to do about Tyler and Angela.

"It all started with only this fishing captain and the use of his boat."

"Now it is almost out of control."

"Nothing is ever out of control," the older man assured Mr. Shalita.

"Then, we kill them all?"

"Exactly, that is why we use expendables. They cost little and are easy to dispose of."

The two men discussed in detail what Tyler and Angela planned to do. They talked of Jonathan's betrayal. It was as if they were doing away with wild animals. It all was to take place in less than four days.

Yahimo Shalita left the meeting. Outside the building he pulled up the collar of his coat to protect him from the cool morning air. He wanted with all his heart to please his cousin back in Tokyo and to be recalled to Japan. He had not seen his family for over two years.

When Shalita turned the first corner heading for his car, from out of the shadows emerged a FBI agent with a special listening device. He carefully stowed the device in its bag and drove back into the city to report to his superior. It had been a long night; he was ready to go home and rest. However, he knew he would have to give a full report as soon as he got to the office. Sometimes he thought his boss lived at the FBI office and never left.

At the same time he was excited about this case. It had so many twists and turns. It had so many varied characters. He wondered how one woman content on revenge could get so many others into the same trouble. He also was anxious to bring down the Japanese underworld working in their region.

"So this Vicki Richards got involved with Jonathan Winston to get even with her husband Tyler? In the process this poor life guard got killed? Prior to this the good captain makes a deal with the Japanese underworld to haul and help sell these three Japanese treasures? Tyler hires this PI who is really part of the Japanese underworld to keep an eye on Vicki? Tyler gets Winston's wife Angela involved to get revenge on both Vicki and Jonathan? It sounds like they're all out to destroy each other?" The head FBI agent tried to sum up the whole situation.

"That's about it," the other agent agreed.

"We need to move quickly or we're going to have a lot of dead bodies on our hands."

"Is anybody innocent in this complicated mess?"

"No, sir. I think each has his/her own devilish motives for what's happening."

"Tomorrow I want to know what your plans are to handle this mess."

"Yes, sir."

The next afternoon an anonymous phone call to the FBI led them to Jonathan Winston's fishing boat. The report said that shots were heard in the area. The agents arrived too late. They found the dead bodies of Vicki Richards and Jonathan Winston and Yahimo Shalita. Witnesses said they saw several Japanese men leave the fishing boat in a hurry and drive away in a waiting car. Nobody could adequately put the pieces of the puzzle together. And nobody knew anything about Tyler and Angela. A week later one witness claimed he saw a man and a woman running from Jonathan Winston's boat. They got on board a speed boat, left the harbor, and, yes, they were carrying a bag of heavy items.

In a newly constructed yacht off the coast of Brazil the newly weds Mr. and Mrs. Tyler and Angela Richards sipped iced tea and feasted on caviar. They had not a care in the world. Angela's children played below deck.

"I can hardly believe how easy this whole thing was." Angela adjusted the sunglasses on her nose.

"I know. It just fell together."

"That PI of yours tried to betray us. He was a crook all along."

"Well, thanks to your husband, he is dead."

"Well, thanks to those Japanese gentlemen, my husband and your wife are dead."

"And we didn't have to kill anybody."

"Nope, all we had to do was to walk in between the killings and take the treasure."

"Aw, the treasure. Now that they're sold, the name Imperial Regalia of Japan sure does have a pretty ring to it, doesn't it?"

Angela sipped her tea and tasted the caviar. "It does. It does."

Tyler got up and started below. "I need to make a few phone calls to get ready for my trip to San Francisco. I have some business to tend to."

"San Francisco. That'll be a nice trip. Can I go?"

"No, not this time."

An Expensive Win

It wasn't until after I lost my mother that I realized how fortunate my life really had been. I was nobody. My parents were nobodies. I came from nowhere. I had no past, present, or future. I had no dreams or goals. I was an empty balloon floating along in the eternity of the universe. I had no education or insight.

I was born in Crooked Creek, Alabama. My mother was a maid for these white folks in Jasper. My daddy cut grass during the day and cleaned the streets at night. I am a Negro. That fact was pointed out to me all my life. I was second class. I was from the wrong side of town. I went to school with all the others Negroes. I almost learned to read. I can write a little bit.

When I turned seventeen, I found out you could join the army if your parents would sign for you. That was back in the sixties. Everybody knows what was going on then. I knew we were at war somewhere, but I had no clue where Viet Nam was. I talked with the recruiter in Jasper. He promised to fix me up. He sure did that.

The recruiter, Sgt Joseph Henry, helped me pass all the tests to join up. The next thing that I really remember is graduating from boot camp and from AIT. I was an infantry soldier on my way to Viet Nam. The third day I found myself on a patrol in the deepest jungles of the planet earth. Nothing in my prior life prepared me for what I experienced over the next four months.

I had never seen a dead person, much less watch a man die right in front of me. In fact I had not seen much blood. However, in Viet Nam I saw many young men die. I saw men with all sorts of body parts blown away. I saw bodies wiggle while the heads lay many feet away. I saw soldiers die from snake bites and poison stakes.

But you know what I realized? Pain hurts whether you're black or white. Blood is red whether you're black or white. Death is being dead whether you're black or white. In those times brothers in combat tend to forget about skin color, being rich or poor, going to college or not finishing high school, etc. Your priorities get all mixed up, or should I say they get straightened out?

Let me tell you what happened the Tuesday of the first week of my fifth month. We were out on a patrol. It had been raining for over two hours. Recon let us know we were in an area where the enemy had been sighted. We were on high alert. We had a new sergeant heading our patrol. It was his third tour in Viet Nam. He was gung ho. He was army all the way to his underwear.

"Arnold, take the point."

"Got it, sarge," I said.

"Move out."

We were about ten miles out from camp. We had two days rest since our last patrol. My M16 needed cleaning, but I needed sleep more. Unlike other soldiers I had no pictures of my family or girlfriend. My family never took pictures, and I had no girlfriend. I had a cigarette stuck under my helmet strap. I started smoking and drinking, but I never got in the groove of using drugs. I'm not sure why; it just never lured me.

"Hey, Arnold, what you thinking about up there?"

"Nothing important," I answered.

"Have you read any of that book I gave you?"

"No." I turned to look back. That was my big mistake. I didn't want to say I had trouble with most of the words in the book.

With my next stride, I stepped on a land mine. It exploded and ripped my left leg off just above the knee. What remained of my severed leg flew up in a nearby tree. I fell to the ground and began to scream. Blood poured out onto the ground, mixing with rain water.

"Spread out and take cover," the sergeant yelled.

We were caught in a cross fire. I was the only one laying out in the open. I tried to crawl to one side and get under some of the huge leaves. The pain was too severe. All I could do was lay there and cringe in pain. Somehow I managed to stop screaming.

"Arnold, just be still. We'll get you as soon as we can."

"I'm not going anywhere," I said, trying to be funny.

Teddy from Mississippi tried to come get me. He took a bullet to the shoulder and one to the head. He lay dead beside me. About half an hour later Max from Texas came after me. He had no better luck. The enemy zeroed in on him. He took a bullet in the back and one in his heart. He lay dead about two feet from me.

"Just lay still, Arnold," I heard someone whispering to me. "We'll be there as soon as we can."

Then the enemy broke through the trees and bushes in front of us. They outnumbered us about twenty-to-one. We didn't have a chance. I decided to play dead. Two Viet Cong soldiers rolled me over and must have thought I was dead. They left me laying there. I was getting very, very weak from blood loss. I must have passed out.

The next thing I remember is waking up aboard a chopper headed for a field hospital. I asked about the patrol. I was told I was the only one that survived. I turned my head and looked out the chopper as we flew over the tree tops. I closed my eyes and wept like a baby. I never figured out why I am alive and they are all dead. I should be dead. They should be alive. That's the truth of the matter.

Over the next three months I had six operations on my leg. Each of the operations left me weaker and weaker. I tried to eat but couldn't keep anything on my stomach. I did not accept the idea that I was alive and the rest of the patrol were all dead. Finally, the surgeon suggested that I speak to the chaplain and to the psychiatrist. The chaplain had been by to visit several times, but I wasn't much in the mood to talk. The next day I was ready.

"Mind if I sit down?"

"No, sir. Please do."

"Col Andrews asked me to come by. He is concerned about you. He said physically you are coming along fine but emotionally you are going down hill."

"Yes, sir. I think I have to agree with him."

"Want to talk about it?"

"Yes, sir."

My family back in Crooked Creek, Alabama was really religious. I had been to several churches with my mother's and daddy's families. My parents did not claim to be part of any particular church. We went when and where it was convenient. As I remember I had never been to a Catholic church. I was a mixed Baptist-Church of Christ-Methodist-hard core Pentecostal, and not a bit of it made sense to me.

"Do you mind telling me about your leg?" the chaplain asked.

I stared at the chaplain. Here was a preacher in an army uniform. He was young, white, fair skinned, and built like an athlete. However, for some reason I felt like he really did care about me. He wore a wedding ring and a great big college ring from the University of Alabama.

"You from Alabama, sir?"

"I was born in Birmingham and grew up in Phenix City."

"Do they draft chaplains, sir?"

"No, I joined because I wanted to."

"They ordered you to Viet Nam?"

"Actually, I volunteered to come here."

"Let me tell you about the patrol, sir."

For about two hours the chaplain sat there beside my bed, and I poured out my heart and my guts. I explained how I didn't want to die and how the others didn't deserve to die. I told in vivid detail how I lost my leg and how the fellows tried to rescue me. I told him I hadn't even spent a whole lot of time thinking about my leg. I would give my other leg to have them all back alive again.

"Do you feel guilty?" the chaplain asked me.

"Yes, sir. In a way."

"You didn't kill the men on that patrol. You would have tried to rescue them if they had been wounded. They wanted to rescue you. That was their decision, and then the enemy overran you all."

"I know that, sir, in my head, but not in my heart." I pointed to my head and then to my heart.

"You know what I think, Arnold?"

"What, sir?"

He picked up his helmet with his dull silver cross on the front. "I think if they could talk to you, they would tell you to get on with your life."

"Do you really think so, sir?"

"I really think so. I know that is what God wants."

The chaplain left. I lay there on that bed and said over and over and over in my mind: get on with my life, get on with my life. Then it hit me. I had lost a leg, but I had not lost my life. I rested my head on the pillow and closed my eyes. For the first time in several days I slept in peace.

The next morning a lady medic came to visit me. Actually, she was a physical therapist. She was black and from Georgia. It was love for me at first sight. When I saw her, I forgot all about my leg.

"Good morning, Mr. Arnold."

"Gooood morning." My eyes were sparkling.

"Are you ready to work on your new leg?"

"Are you going to help me?"

"I am."

"Then I am ready and willing."

She laughed. I laughed. She sat down on the chair beside my bed. She carried a clip board with papers. She started asking me all kinds of questions. The questions took me back to that last patrol. All of a sudden I was down again.

"I know this is not pleasant, but it will help me help you. Okay?"

She stayed with me about forty-five minutes. Before she left, she asked me about my family. I asked her about her family. We had a lot in common. I think it was then that she really took an interest in me. Her mom was a maid, too. Her daddy was a janitor at one of the local schools. It seemed that cleaning and scrubbing ran in both our families.

As she was leaving, I asked her, "What is your name?"

"Maggie. Maggie Heartstone. I will see you later this afternoon."

"I'll be right here, waiting on you."

For some reason that afternoon after lunch I took a long look at myself. I looked at my past, my present, and my future. I always thought it all was a big fat zero. Something about joining the army and going to war changes a man. Seeing men die. Getting blown up myself opened my eyes. I think I started seeing things clearer when the chaplain was there in the hospital with me.

Don't get me wrong. I didn't have some religious experience. I just came to realize the significance in what happened to me in the last year or so. I joined the army before I was drafted. I volunteered to go to Viet Nam. I offered myself up on the altar of my country. I was a living sacrifice. However, the point IS I was living.

Over the next several months I learned to walk on an artificial leg. I got pretty good at it as a matter of fact. As time passed, I got better acquainted with Maggie. I explained to her that I was going back to Alabama and going back to school. I wasn't sure what I would study or where, but I was a changed man. I was going to make something out of the rest of my life.

Maggie was due to get out of the army in seven months. She planned to go back to her folks in Georgia. We talked of getting back together once we were both in the United States. I was excited about the future. There was hope and a sense of peace. For once I was happy and satisfied, with anticipation of what was facing me in the future.

The day before I left to fly back home, Maggie and I went out for supper. We went to a nice Hawaiian restaurant. Really I know nothing about Hawaii except that it is pretty beyond description. I never saw anything like it in Alabama. We ate at the Aloha Today. I knew nothing about Hawaiian food. I called ahead to make reservations and also asked the owner to pick out something he thought was appropriate for two black soldiers from the USA.

The taxi driver let us out at the front door. I made arrangements for him to pick us up later at nine o'clock. A one legged man can get around, but it is some different from jumping into the world with the two legs the good Lord gave us. I was getting used to using the artificial leg. In fact, it no longer embarrassed me.

As we walked up to the front door, Maggie said, "Arnold, I'm going to miss you. You are undoubtedly the best patient I ever worked with."

"Why, thank you, Miss Heartstone. You make it easy to be such a patient."

We entered and the waiter took us to our table. A man played the piano off to the side. There was a small band playing with him softly in the background. I never danced, but the urge came over me then. Several couples danced out on the floor in front of the man playing the piano. It looked like all were enjoying themselves. I decided against trying to dance. Why make a fool of myself?

"This is lovely. Thank you for bringing me here."

"You are most welcome."

"Are you anxious to see your parents?"

"In a way. They keep writing about me being a hero."

"You are a hero."

"I'm not a hero. I'm just a lucky SOB."

Maggie looked beautiful. She wore a pink dress and matching earrings. Her neck was as the carving of a goddess on stone. Her face was bright, and her eyes filled the sockets as the ornaments of a classical crown. She smiled, and the whole world stopped for a time to smile back at her. She was beautiful. She brightened up a room that was already full of lesser stars.

"Maggie, I think I'm falling in love with you."

"I know I'm already in love with you, Arnold."

"I've never had a girlfriend. I never even kissed a girl, and certainly never went to bed with one."

"Arnold, you need to know that I was married."

"Was?"

"Yes, WAS."

"Then it's over?"

"It was over before it hardly started."

"What do you mean?"

"Bobby was a soldier, too. We got married after he finished boot camp. He was killed in Viet Nam six weeks later."

"I'm sorry to hear that."

"He stepped on a land mine, but it didn't just blow a leg off. It blew his body into five ragged parts. They brought all the pieces back. It was terrible."

"How did you get over that?"

"It wasn't easy. I went to lots of counseling and did a lot of praying."

"I really am sorry."

"It's not your fault; we all have our burdens to bear."

"When you get back to the states, may I see you again?"

"I would like that," Maggie said.

The next morning I left for the United States and then back home to Alabama. In New Jersey I picked up a ticket for a mega lottery. I knew I wouldn't win; I just thought it would be a good game to play. The ticket cost me three dollars. Three days later I found out that I had won five million dollars. Again my life made another turn, and not really for the better.

I arrived back in Crooked Creek, Alabama not the poor, ignorant Negro that left, but a man with the world at his finger tips. Everybody who was somebody either knew me or wanted to know me. They all had my interests in mind and wanted to save me from those evil predators out in the world who were out to get my money.

Momma and daddy hardly recognized me. I walked with a limp. I had lost what little weight I had when I went into the army. They couldn't at all relate to millions of dollars.

"What do you mean you won all that money?" momma asked.

"I bought this ticket at a small grocery store on the way home."

"It's got to be a mistake. We never had no money," daddy said.

"I'm thirsty," I said. "Let's have some cold water and let me explain."

Momma brought us a pitcher of iced water. The fan was running in the window beside the kitchen table. Daddy wore his work overalls. Momma had on a large white apron over her blue dress. They both looked fit for their age. Everybody was more interested in my money than my missing leg. I saw momma watch me as I walked over to sit down at the table.

"Yes, momma. It really is true. I lost that leg, and I'm wearing an artificial one. I still get around good, but I have some horrible memories."

"My poor boy." Momma pulled me close to her chest and held me there for what seemed like a long time. "I love you, son, and I'm very proud of you."

"I know, momma."

I pulled away. "I know what I'm going to do. I'm going to get us something special to drink. Something to help us celebrate getting back together."

"Like what? I got a fresh pot of tea making."

"I'll show you, mom."

This was before the whole world knew I lived in Crooked Creek, Alabama. There were only a few reporters outside the house. I ignored them and headed for the super market. I was going after some champagne and Irish Whiskey. I knew about champagne, but I had only heard of Irish Whiskey. I wanted to introduce momma and daddy to the finer things of life, like I was the one in the know. Boy, did I have a lot to learn.

The manager of the grocery store recognized me and came out of the office to shake my hand and tell me how happy he was that I had won the money. Then he said he was sorry about my leg and thanked me for serving in the army. He had been in the army in World War Two. He said we were comrades and told me I could have all the drinks I wanted, free. That was the beginning of the end.

Back at the house, I had to coax momma and daddy into drinking anything but water and tea. Once they had the taste down, momma really liked it. In fact, she liked it too much.

The next morning when I got up, I found momma sitting at the table drinking more Irish Whiskey. I didn't make the connection at the time. I was proud that I had started them on a new lifestyle.

"Take it easy on that, momma," I said.

"Don't worry. I only want a little sip. It tastes good."

"I know. It took me awhile, but I admit it really is good."

I ordered a brochure about a cruise to the Bahamas. That brochure came with the first letter from Maggie. I was happy to get the letter. Maggie told me she was getting out of the army early and wanted to meet me as soon as possible. One of Maggie's patients had died and the army felt she had spent enough time with Viet Nam casualties.

She didn't mention the lottery money. I knew she was interested in me and not my money. She cared for me before I had any money. I wrote back and asked if she would want to take a cruise with me and my family.

We agreed to meet in West Palm Beach and take the cruise ship from there. Momma and daddy were excited. I was ready to be back with Maggie. I took momma and daddy to Birmingham to go shopping. We had to be sneaky because of the money hungry folks and the reporters. I had already hired six men to watch out for us. I had bought a new Cadillac and hired a driver. He knew his way around and knew how to outrun and to evade unwanted intruders.

Momma bought several new dresses along with a hat, matching purses and shoes, even new underwear and gloves. Daddy bought several pairs of pants and short sleeve shirts and a jacket that matched and a new pair of shoes and three pair of socks. Momma found a way to bring a bottle of Irish Whiskey with her. I caught her sipping a couple of times. She was getting secretive and avoiding eye-contact. Still at the time I didn't think anything about her drinking. I never worried about my parents; they always worried about me.

I sent Maggie five hundred dollars and told her to use it as she pleased to prepare for our trip. I didn't know what she got until we were together in Florida. To say the least, she used the money wisely; she looked beautiful.

The time finally came for us to leave for Florida. We were not in a hurry. I got the new driver to drive us to Florida. We stopped frequently along the way. I never realized how often momma went to the bathroom. I didn't realized how much momma was drinking. I never realized that a black man could be accepted into a white man's world if he had the money to justify the admittance. It is true: money talks, and it talks loud and clear. If I had only seen what all this was doing to momma. Daddy took it all with such ease.

Maggie met us at the ship. Momma did not like her from the start. We had agreed to meet on the landing. The driver unloaded the car and put the baggage on a strolling cart. I pushed it toward the check-in area. Then I saw Maggie. She was more gorgeous than I could have imagined. She had her long hair in a pony tail and looked like a black Shirley Temple. I was proud she had come.

On the other hand, Momma was totally different. I introduced them all.

"Maggie, this is my momma and daddy. This is Maggie. She is the lady who helped me through the hard times of getting use to this new leg."

"It's a pleasure to meet you," Maggie said.

Daddy said, "You're prettier than he said you were."

Momma said nothing. She turned and walked over to one of her suitcases and tried to look like she was securing it better.

"Forgive her, Maggie. This new leg and this new money are all strange to her." He went over and stood by momma.

I heard momma, and I know Maggie did, say to daddy, "That girl's not getting my boy. It will take more than her likes to take him away."

"She's not trying to take our boy away."

"Yes, she is. That's the only reason she's on this trip. Just look: a man with a fake leg and millions of dollars. What do you think that adds up to?"

"I think it could add up to love and a happy life for the both of them."

"Over my dead body," momma said.

I spoke up and said, "Let's check in and get aboard. This is going to be fun for us all. We all need to get away and enjoy the ocean and the sun and the tranquility."

"That's right, son," daddy agreed.

"It's just a waste of time," momma replied.

We checked our baggage and secured our boarding passes and started for the elevator leading up to the gangplank. It was higher than anything I had seen in the army. I was a little apprehensive; I never did care for heights. After boarding one of the officers took us to our cabins. I had booked three cabins. Mine and Maggie's were both seaward and had portholes. The setting sun looked alive and gallant through the glass. Momma and daddy's was next to ours, but not seaward and had no portholes. Our trip was to last five days. However, circumstances cut it short.

As soon as we were settled, I took Maggie for a walk around the ship. It was so big and so impressive. From the inside you couldn't tell you were on a ship. We visited the pool and the theater and the dining room. I should say we visited the pools, the theaters, and the dining rooms. It was almost overwhelming. Neither Maggie nor I had ever seen anything to compare with it.

When we were on the upper deck, I stopped at the railing and looked out to sea. Maggie rested right up against me. I slipped my arm around her waist. She snuggled closer. I did the most natural thing: I turned to look her in the face and kissed her square on the lips. She was not at all surprised or unwilling.

"I missed you since I left the hospital," I said.

"All I have thought of is you. I am glad the army let me out early. I was about to go out of my mind missing you."

"Maggie, I love you."

"I love you, Arnold."

I kissed her again and said, "Let's go tour the ship some more. This is all new to me."

"Let me ask you a question, please."

"Of course."

"Why doesn't your mother like me?"

"I don't think its momma; I think it's the alcohol. I plan to have a long talk with her when we get back. I also plan to have her get whatever help she needs. I have heard of people reacting to alcohol like momma is, but I never saw anybody."

"What can I do to get on her good side?"

"I don't know; I just want you on my good side." I smiled.

"Has she always been this way?"

"No. Actually, it's all my fault and the money I won."

"How's that?"

"When I got home, I wanted to get a drink to celebrate.   After momma's first drink, that was all it took."

"You mean all this just started?"

"Yes. I mean just started."

"Oh, Arnold, you've got to help her and stop this."

"I know, and I will, when we get back from this trip."

The ship pulled out that night. I slept well. The next day we were well out to sea. I had never seen such beautiful sights as the sun bouncing off the ocean waves, the large fish flying along our side, and water as far as I could see. What a delightful difference from the war in Viet Nam. I almost forgot I had a fake leg and how I got it in the first place.

That evening we ate in a formal dining room. We all dressed up. I have to admit if I did not know everyone before I saw them dressed up, I would not have recognized them. We were fit to appear in the movies. Daddy looked the best to me. He had never worn a suit, much less a tux. Mother was simply a darling. However, Maggie could have chosen her pick of any man on earth. I sure was happy she was with me.

We ate at a table with a full sparkling white linen cloth. We could have skipped all the plates and bowls and simply eaten off the table cloth. We had steak and lobster. We had champagne. I kept an eye on momma. I thought she behaved herself. We had the best rolls on planet earth. In a way I wish that meal could have lasted forever. I know I will never forget it.

The waiter served us like we were royalty. He was always there. No plate or glass ever went empty for long. Toward the end of the meal he asked me if I would like to try some escargot. I said certainly.

"What is it?" I asked Maggie.

"Snails."

"You're kidding?"

"Nope, but I think you'll like them."

"He won't like that trash," momma blurted in, her words slurred.

"Let me try, momma."

"She thinks she's so high and mighty just because she knows what that dumb word means."

"I asked her, momma."

"That woman's nothing but a slut and a whore."

"Momma, tell her you're sorry and you didn't mean it."

"I'm not sorry, and I meant exactly what I said."

"In that case, if you'll excuse us, we'll go somewhere else for the time being."

"No! You stay here. I'm going back to my room. I've had all of this trip I can stand."

Daddy was so embarrassed. I felt sorry for him. He loved momma. He and I both knew she was not acting like herself. It was more and more apparent that I had made a mistake by introducing momma to alcohol. Momma left the table, after throwing her cloth napkin down on the table. Daddy looked helpless.

"She'll be okay. I'll get her help as soon as we get back home," I said.

"As far as I know, she never before even tasted wine or beer or anything like that. Now she wants that Irish Whiskey all the time."

"I better see that she gets to the room," I said.

"No, I'll go," Maggie said. "You stay here and talk with your daddy."

"You sure?"

"Yes, I won't let her know I'm following her. I'll just make sure she gets back to the room okay."

Maggie left Daddy and me. We continued our conversation. We talked about momma and about Viet Nam and about my artificial leg. It was one of the best talks a father and son could have. I felt closer to him than ever before. I knew he loved momma and was awfully worried about her.

Maggie came back to the dining room some thirty minutes later. A worried look covered her face. "I can't find her," she said.

"What do you mean?" Daddy asked.

"After I left here, I never found her. I went all the way to the cabin with no sight of her. I even knocked on the door. There was no answer. I asked a couple of other tourists if they saw her. Nobody saw her between here and the cabin. I went out on deck and went to the cabin that way. I am worried about her."

"I am, too," Daddy said.

"Let's go look around, and then we'll tell one of the officers," I said.

We spent the next forty-five minutes looking for momma. She was not in the cabin. There was no trace of her. Finally, we gave up and reported her missing to the ship's crew. They did a quick search, without any success. The captain called for a state of emergency and stopped the ship. They did a search of the waters.

The captain decided to trace the ship's path and look for momma. About two hours later someone saw something floating in the water. A diver went in to check the object. He called back for the captain to have the doctor on hand. He pulled the object to the lower deck of the ship. There others of the crew helped him bring it aboard.

It was momma. She was dead. A shark had attacked her and bitten off both her legs. It was almost more than I could stand. The doctor would not let us see momma's body. It was that bad. Daddy cried. I cried. I think Maggie tried to cry. I took Daddy back to his cabin. The doctor gave him a shot, and he slept the rest of the night.

I took Maggie back to her cabin. We went in and sat down on the bunk. On the table was a fresh bouquet of flowers. The scent filled the room. I started to bawl like a baby. I beat on my leg and screamed, "I hate you. I hate you."

"I'm sorry about your momma," Maggie said. She put her arms around me and held me close.

"I wish I'd never joined the army. I wish I'd never heard of Viet Nam. I wish I had not lost my leg. And I wish I'd never won all that damn money."

Maggie kissed me on the cheek. "I love you, Arnold. I'm so sorry about your momma. Your daddy's been so sweet. Now, I hope he doesn't try to get in our way."

It wasn't until later that I learned the doctor had questions regarding momma's death. In fact, the captain had one of his officers make sure the police were waiting at the pier as we pulled in the next day. We all believed she was drunk and fell overboard. However, the doctor and captain knew something we didn't.

Pass Me Not

Phil Slusher was a nobody who always wanted to be a somebody. He wanted to be part of a team; he wanted to belong. He wanted to be wanted. To other people he did not matter. Phil was small, insignificant, and unwanted. That was until he met a kid about to die from birth defects.

In the third grade his teacher had the class write and perform a play. Phil wrote a scene for the play which the teacher rejected. Phil wanted to play one of the children who lived by the sea, but the teacher picked another boy.

In the sixth grade his teacher had the whole class enter an essay contest. Phil went home and wrote a short article about the monkeys in the city zoo. The teacher told Phil that his essay was too long and rejected it before he could enter it in the contest.

In the tenth grade his home room teacher had the students sell candy to raise money for a local charity event. The other students made so much fun of Phil that the teacher decided he did not have the ability to sell candy and did not include him in the project.

In his senior year the high school formed a debate team. The first debate centered on gun control and the U.S. Constitution. Phil went to the school and the city libraries to do research. The other students and the faculty sponsors would not even let Phil try out for the team.

However, there was one school counselor who liked and wanted to encourage Phil to go on to college. One day Phil dropped by Mrs. Michael's office.

"Where are you planning to apply to go to college?" Mrs. Michael asked Phil.

"I don't think I'll apply anywhere."

"Why not?"

"I'm not college material."

"Phil, why do you say that?"

"I don't have the grades. I haven't been involved in any extracurricular activities. I have nothing going for me in school and no reason to go on in school."

Mrs. Michael had known Phil all through high school. She knew how he tried and was beaten down at every turn. She really liked him and felt sorry for him. She also knew there was a lot of truth to what he had just said.

"What will you do?" she asked.

"I think I'll go into the military."

"You know there is a war going on, and chances are good you'll end up in Iraq."

"I know, but that's part of being in the army. There's always that chance."

"Yes, you're right. What do your parents think?"

"I don't really think it matters to them; they're ready for me to get out of the house."

After graduation Phil enlisted in the US Army and found himself in basic training and then in advanced infantry training. Within eight months he was attached to a unit on its way to Iraq.

Early one sunny morning Phil was checking cars and trucks along a roadblock south of Bagdad. A suicide bomber drove up in a truck and set off the bomb. Phil was so close that the blast threw him up against a brick wall and crushed his back. Fifteen of the other soldiers were killed.

Phil spent over a year in the army hospital before being discharged from the hospital and from the army, with a piddling monthly disability check.

With no place else to go, Phil returned to his home town, wearing a back brace and with a limp in his walk. His parents reluctantly let him come back home, thinking they might be stuck with him the rest of their lives.

Two months after Phil returned home, one late afternoon he went for a slow walk around his neighborhood. The traffic seemed busier than usual. He stopped and chatted with the group of kids playing baseball in the vacant corner lot.

"Mister, what happened to you," one of the little boys asked.

Phil simply shrugged and said, "I was in an accident."

"Oh," he replied.

"Mister, can you pitch the ball to us while we practice batting."

"I think I might be able to do that."

Three boys and a girl lined up around the batter's box while Phil stood halfway between the pitcher's mound and home plate. His first six pitches the ball did not make it to home plate.

"Come on, mister, you can throw harder than that. We are not babies."

Phil pitched ball to the kids for about thirty minutes, until his arms began to hurt. He put the ball down on the pitcher's mound and thanked them all for letting him play. He saw a boy watching them from the edge of the field. He walked over to him. The boy had blue eyes and red hair. He had a crutch under each arm.

"Howdy," Phil said.

"Hi," came the reply.

"You play any sports?" Phil asked.

"Just chess and video games."

"I play chess," Phil said, excitedly.

"Do you like video games?"

"Yes, but I'm not very good."

"You want to go play?"

"Where?"

"I live just down the street. My mom would let you come in. She always has cookies and milk when I get home."

"Sure, let's go play. Sure it's okay with your mom?"

"I think so; we'll ask her."

Phil followed his new friend home. His mother was sitting on the swing that hung from a big oak tree in the front yard. She got up when she saw her son coming. She waved and said hello. "Who's your new friend?" Right away she noticed Phil's brace and limp.

"This is Phil. He was playing ball with the kids over at the lot. We got to talking about chess and video games. Mind if he comes in and plays with me?"

"Hello, Phil. My name is Judy Wright. I am Abe's mother."

"It's nice to meet you, Mrs. Wright. I'm Phil Slusher. Looks like Abe and I have a lot in common."

"Yes, it does. Sure, come in and spend some time with Abe."

Once inside the house Abe and Phil sat down in the living room and played a couple of games of chess. Each won a game. Mrs. Wright brought them milk and cookies, just like Abe said she would. Then they played video games for about an hour. Abe got up and went to the bathroom.

While Abe was gone, Mrs. Wright said, "Abe has a birth defect. What happened to you, if I may ask?" She spoke with care and concern.

"I was in the army stationed in Iraq. A suicide bomber drove a truck right up to the road block I was working and blew himself up. I was lucky; fifteen others were killed."

"I'm sorry to hear that. How are you doing?"

"I have good and bad days. How is Abe doing?"

"He has good and bad days. Actually, he's not doing well, and we have not told him. He doesn't have too long to live."

"I'm sorry to hear that. Is there anything I can do?"

"You're already doing it. He needs a friend and somebody to give him some attention."

"Mrs. Wright, I can do that. I wish I'd had a friend and someone to give me some time and attention when I was Abe's age."

"How is that?"

"Let's just say that Abe and I are like two birds in the same cage."

The Neglected Grave

Mr. Jacob Tarpley owned and managed Grace Mountain Memorial Gardens just north of Birmingham, Alabama. The cemetery was peaceful, and most local people preferred it over other cemeteries in the county. Two weeks prior Mr. Tarpley buried the daughter of Mr. Johnson Miles, the owner of a local hardware store. Circumstances surrounding the daughter's death were questionable. The funeral and the burial were closed to the public. Speculation circulated as to what was said and done at both.

The grave had sunk at least ten inches at the head and at the foot. Mr. Tarpley was not at all in favor personally of repairing the grave, and he could get nobody else to fill in where the grave sank, including his own two cemetery workers. Gossip had it that the daughter had been a witch and promised to return to life within three weeks after her death.

One evening at the dinner table Mrs. Tarpley asked her husband, "What's to become of the witch's grave? I hear it's sinking more and more. People can already see the vault."

"I suppose I'm going to have to go and fill it in myself; I can't get anyone else to do it. It is almost like that grave has control over this whole community."

"Is that possible?" Cherry, their fifteen-year-old daughter, asked. Cherry walked, talked, and acted like her mother, including her intrusive and stubborn nature.

"I'm afraid so. People in this county are mighty superstitious."

"Pass me the bread, please," Mrs. Tarpley said, trying to change the subject.

Mr. Tarpley sat at one end of the table and his wife at the other. Cherry always sat in the middle between her parents. Most of the food found its way to Mr. Tarpley's end of the table before the meal was over. He eased the bread over toward Cherry, and she handed it to her mother.

"Once I saw Mr. Miles' daughter out in their back yard. She didn't look much older than I am," Cherry said.

Mrs. Tarpley looked at Cherry and demanded, "What were you doing over there?"

"It was a dare. One afternoon some of the girls dared me to go by."

"And you fell for that?" her daddy asked.

"It was a dare, just a joke."

"Did she see you?"

"Yes, she did."

"Did she speak to you?"

"First she waved at me and then she motioned for me to come to her."

"Surely, you didn't go in their yard?"

"Yes, mother, I went in the yard. I even sat in the swing and talked with her."

"What did she say?"

"She told me her name was Temple."

"Temple Miles, a mild name for a witch, if you ask me," offered Mr. Tarpley.

There came a knock at the front door. Cherry pushed back her chair and started to get up and go check the door. Mr. Tarpley motioned her back down. "Maybe I'd better go see who is there."

However, before Mr. Tarpley reached the door, the knob turned and Mr. Miles let himself in. He was breathing heavily and sweating, his face white and constricted in fright. "I'm so very sorry to barge in like this, but I need your help right now."

"What's the matter, Mr. Miles, you look horrible?" Mr. Tarpley asked.

"It's the grave. I haven't been to the cemetery today, but somebody told me the grave is open, and the whole vault is exposed. We must close the grave right now before the sun sets and the moon rises."

"Man, what are you talking about?"

"I have no time to explain. I have a car outside. Call your men and tell them to meet us and have that backhoe of yours at the grave." Mr. Miles sounded and looked desperate.

"Okay. Just calm down. It's all going to be okay."

"We'll see; we must hurry. This whole community is in danger."

"Can I go, daddy?" Cherry asked.

"NO!" shouted Mr. Miles. "It is far too dangerous."

"Yes, come on. You need to see how foolishly some people can get worked up." He told his wife to call his workers and have them and the backhoe waiting.

"Don't take the girl. I'm warning you, sir. Leave her here at home."

Mr. Tarpley didn't listen and let Cherry go to the cemetery with them. The sun was low over the woods and hills. A bright orange haze covered the sky. The sun was no longer visible. The moon was not yet up, but the North Star and (perhaps it was) Venus were up high in the sky.

"Hurry!" Mr. Miles commanded. "We must beat the sun."

Temple was buried in the upright monument section back by the woods. When the car turned into the cemetery, the two men and the backhoe were nowhere to be seen.

"Where's your crew?" asked Mr. Miles.

"They should already be here. Drive on around to the barn. We'll see if they are there."

They passed by Temple's grave on the way to the barn. Fresh dirt lay piled at the foot of her grave. The monument at the head lay toppled on its back. A fine mist rose up out of the grave.

"What's going on?" asked Mr. Tarpley.

"Oh, no, surely we're not too late."

"Here's comes Buster and Buddy with the backhoe," shouted Cherry.

"Thankfully. Now let's get this grave covered before all hell breaks loose." Again, one could almost feel the terror in Mr. Miles' voice.

Getting out of the car Mr. Tarpley noticed the eerie silence of the cemetery. Besides the voices and the noise of the backhoe, the silence was heavy and overbearing. The whole world seemed to be in a deep coma.

Buster and Buddy both rode on the backhoe as it came off the pavement and onto the dirt and grass of the garden. Even from a distance it was apparent they did not want to be at the cemetery. Before they reached the grave, the moon came up and a pale blue darkness covered the area. The sun with its orange haze disappeared, and the clouds traveled over a black sky. Here and there a star began to twinkle. One could see the moon's reflection in the nearby pond. They heard fish splashing in the pond and crickets in the woods and the breeze in the trees. The earth returned to life.

An owl hooted, and Mr. Miles knew they arrived too late. He stopped a few feet from the grave and looked down. The grave was open, the vault lid to the side, the casket bare, and no sign of Temple.

Mr. Miles sat down hard on one of the monuments and began to cry, almost wailing. The whole affair amazed Cherry. She had no idea what was going on. Surely somebody had stolen the body and was trying to trick and scare the local people, she thought.

Tarpley became angry and demanded, "Okay, man, give it to me straight; what's with it here?"

Mr. Miles looked up and wiped tears from his eyes. "I don't understand it completely; I will try to explain."

Cherry noticed something white just beyond the tree line. It looked like a dress. Then it gave off a soft yellow glow. The men were too busy talking to see what went on behind them. Cherry felt this drawing sensation from the glowing dress. As she tiptoed toward the object, she suddenly realized it was Temple, waving after her. Cherry felt faint then curious as to what was really there.

Mr. Miles continued, "Temple found this old manuscript in a trunk up in our attic. It has been there for years. The trunk had not been opened for I don't know how long. It was my grandmother's. She was from the old country in Germany. She learned English but preferred her native German language. She always wanted to go back home."

The closer Cherry got to Temple the more her feelings changed from fright to excitement. She could not understand or explain these feelings. Then came a sense of fulfillment and peace. She was being drawn like a magnet. The light surrounding Temple was like what Cherry imagined the light to be on baby Jesus in the manger: something special and very different; something extraterrestrial.

Mr. Miles paused to take a deep breath; he was getting tired and felt like nobody in the whole world would believe the story he was about to share for the first time.

"What's all that got to do with the trunk and the manuscript?" asked Mr. Tarpley.

"It's all out now; there's no use trying to hide it any longer."

Temple waved to Cherry. "Come here, my dear. I have a wonderful and beautiful gift for you. It will make you happy the rest of your life."

Cherry could no longer hear the two men talking behind her. She was totally focused and controlled by Temple.

"Tell me, man. What's this all about?" Mr. Tarpley urged.

"Grandmother was a witch; no, really she was a queen vampire."

Cherry stood right in front of Temple. The glow had died out. All Cherry saw was the snarl on Temple's face and those two long teeth sticking out down over her lower lip. In a split second Temple had Cherry on her back on the ground. Temple pulled Cherry's hair back exposing her slender, smooth neck. Something inside Cherry screamed, and just as suddenly she actually screamed out loud. The noise woke Cherry from the trance, and it startled Temple, who transposed herself into a bat and flew off.

"What was that?" Tarpley turned and didn't see Cherry. "Where is Cherry?"

"I told you not to bring your daughter; I warned you."

"Help me find her."

"Daddy!" Cherry cried out. She crawled out of the woods on her hands and knees. Her hair was a mess; her dress was torn. Blood trickled down her neck. She was frightened and panting.

"Cherry! Are you okay; what happened?" Tarpley knelt beside his daughter, and then he sat down beside her.

Miles was not as fast reaching the wood's edge. He stopped and looked at the two on the ground. "Is she okay? Check her neck."

"What?" Tarpley asked.

"I said check your daughter's neck for blood and puncture wounds."

Cherry lay on her back with her head in her daddy's lap. Tarpley brushed back the hair, and there he saw two small holes and fresh blood oozing. The look on his face told Miles all he needed to know.

"I told you to leave her at home!" Miles said.

"What is this? What does it mean?" Tarpley asked.

Before Miles could answer, Cherry's eyes popped open; two canine-like teeth stuck out of her upper mouth down over her lower lip. Tarpley instinctively pushed her head away and jumped up off the ground. Miles pulled on him and then pushed him on away from the woods toward the car.

"Is this real?" Tarpley asked, as if he existed in some kind of dream world.

"Again, I told you to leave the girl at home. This curse is especially directed toward the younger females, those under 20 years old."

As the two men started to get into the car, two black bats circled over them and flew off into the wooded area.

'What will I say to Cherry's mother?' Tarpley asked himself.

"Alright, Miles, is this some kind of joke or stunt? What's going on? What are you up to?"

The two workers left the cemetery as soon as Tarpley said they could. Miles drove the car out of the cemetery and back toward town. He stopped at an old truck stop.

"Let's go in here, and I'll explain all I understand."

The two men entered the café. There was only one other customer, sitting way back at a corner table, drinking coffee. He didn't even look up. Miles and Tarpley sat at a table up front. They ordered coffee. Miles was out of breath, and Tarpley was sweating.

"Are you two alright?" the waitress asked.

"Yea, sure. We just need to talk."

"Well, you look like both of you just saw a ghost."

"Something like that," Miles replied flatly.

The waitress shrugged and walked away. She returned periodically to refill their cups. At one point the waitress screamed and dropped the clear glass coffee pot; she stood there pointing at the front window. A bat sat on the window ledge looking into the café. Then another bat joined the first. When the waitress dropped the coffee pot, they flew away.

The owner came out from the back to calm down his worker.

"Tell me, again, about the trunk, the curse, and your grandmother."

"I can tell you all I know and understand. We always knew our grandmother was strange and different in so many ways. I never really knew until now that she was a vampire. I thought they appeared only in novels and the old movies. I assure you they are real. My grandmother got the curse as a young lady, about sixteen. There are only two ways to get the curse: reading the magic words or being bitten by someone with the curse. And that's what happened to our daughters. My daughter put the curse on herself; then she bit your daughter."

"What happened to your daughter? How did she die?" Tarpley asked.

"She killed herself."

"Why? How?"

"She started reading the old manuscripts of my grandmother. I used to wonder why she spent so much time in the attic. Now I know, and far too late."

"How did such old rotten pages affect her so?"

"The more she read, the more she understood, and the more she believed what she read."

The waitress brought them fresh coffee and two lemon pastries. She said, "I want to ask you to forgive me awhile ago for getting scared, screaming, and dropping the coffee pot."

"That's okay; we all get nervous at times," Tarpley replied.

"Yes, but bats, right here on our window. I just know what I hear about them and about those vampires. Of course, everybody knows there really are no vampires."

"Of course," Miles said.

"Of course," Tarpley agreed.

The waitress left, and Miles continued his story.

"But why did she kill herself?"

"To see if the curse was true. She read the magic poems, and she believed. That's really all there is to it. She put the curse on herself and killed herself to see if she would really turn into a vampire."

"And she did!"

"And she did. In fact, we now have two vampires on our hands."

"What are we going to do? Is there any hope or cure for our daughters?"

"I suppose," said Miles, "that we could read the manuscripts and see if there is any way to reverse the curse. If not, we will have to destroy them. Hopefully, before they infect any other young ladies."

Tarpley looked hurt and sorrowful. He needed a long cry. He had lost a daughter, and his wife didn't know a thing about it. "How could we destroy them?"

"We could decapitate them. We could incinerate them. We could drive a stake into their hearts."

"Or we could go back to your house and read the manuscripts."

"Let's go!" Miles said, almost shouting.

At Miles' house the two men found Mrs. Miles waiting for her husband to return and still worrying about her daughter, although she was almost at the point of giving up. Tarpley noticed that Mrs. Miles looked much older and thinner than the last time he saw her.

"We were too late," Miles said to his wife almost apologetically.

"I knew it." She burst into tears.

"I'm so sorry for your loss," Tarpley said, trying to give meaning to his presence.

Before, Mrs. Miles had not even seen Mr. Tarpley. "No, tell me not your daughter, too?" Mrs. Miles' whole body shook as she cried and pointed at Tarpley in sorrow.

"We don't have time for all this," Miles demanded. "We must get upstairs and see if we can decipher the manuscript to reverse the curse. Leave us alone for awhile, please."

Miles led Tarpley through the house to the back stairs that circled up to the attic. A long string attached to a switch turned on the attic light. Miles pulled hard on the string, and the light came on. Both men climbed the stairs. The attic smelt musty and felt dead, drab and shut up; the colors all dark, mostly loud blue and black. The old chest set in the center of the attic, the top open. It appeared as if someone had just rummaged through the chest's contents.   The open manuscript lay on the floor.

"That's it," Miles said, pointing to the tattered collection of papers.

"Let's get with it, man. We don't have all night," Tarpley answered.

Miles picked up the book, and Tarpley noticed the title on front: <u>An Introduction to the State of Feminine Vampires</u>, Translated from the Original German. It was published in London, England in 1796.

Fortunately, it had a table of contents. Chapter eight was called "How to Reverse All the Curses". It started on page 169. Miles opened the manuscript to that page and began to read out loud its contents. It gave a brief summary of each curse and then a detailed way to reverse that curse. The seventh curse in that chapter was "The New Curse for Young Ladies in the New World."

"That must be it," Tarpley interjected.

"It must be."

The translators left all the magic formulas in the original German. As Miles continued to read, he noticed a smudge where someone had changed eight words in the magic formula. Neither of the two men knew a word of German, but Miles learned to read German words as a child, without comprehending any of it. Miles started reading the words.   His voice crackled, and Tarpley pulled at his fingers nervously, hoping this would actually work. Miles stumbled over most of the words. It didn't sound like any German Tarpley had ever heard.

Miles stopped and looked over at Tarpley. He said, "I think this is where the curse is to be reversed." He continued babbling in German. He finished and put the manuscript on top of the trunk. "I guess all we can do is wait."

It wasn't long until a flurry of blue-reddish smoke began circling the attic. Lightening and thunder followed. From the circling smoke came Tarpley's daughter Cherry. Everything about her appeared fresh and pure. She wore the dress she had on at the cemetery, and it looked brand new. Her skin, even around her neck, was soft and clear, like a baby's.

Tarpley rushed over to his daughter and said, "Cherry, are you okay?"

"Sure, daddy. Where are we; what's going on?"

Miles expected his daughter to come out of the circling smoke. He even called out to her, "Temple, are you there? Come on out."

Nothing happened. Miles began to grow restless, but then a young woman did come out of the smoke. She looked to be about seventeen years old. She wore a long formal black dress, her hair dark, long, and draping down her back. An ugly reddish-brown scar raked across her neck.

Right away something about her seemed familiar to Miles.

"Dear, I knew you would read the lines as I had changed them. Thank you, because now I am back on earth, young and full of energy and unstoppable."

"Grandmama, is that you?"

"Nobody else, dear. The queen of the vampires, back to do her duty to her fullest. And nobody will ever stop me now. I will gather an army of young females and turn them all into vampires."

"What about Temple, Grandmama?"

"Your daughter, my dear, was sacrificed for the good of the cause. The same will happen to the daughter of your friend, Mr. Tarpley. Now I must be about my business." At that point her face snarled up and two canine teeth stuck out her mouth over her lower lip.

Tarpley looked over at his daughter and yelled, "Run, Cherry, run!"

Before Cherry could move, Grandmama turned herself into a bat and flew out of the attic. She screamed back at the three in the attic, "Good-bye for now, simple earthlings. I will be back soon, when pretty young Cherry is alone. You can count on it."

Let's Get Together

Paul Preston served in the US Army Special Forces during the Viet Nam War. He was on special assignment in North Viet Nam when he was captured by three families who were civilians used by the enemy in covert ways. In this case their assignment was to find Paul Preston and get rid of him. The families decided to have fun with him before killing him.

That day the sun blared down with extreme heat. Bugs were everywhere. Snakes waited under every rock. Paul Preston was out of ammo. His water was used up two days ago. His rations had been bugs and roots for the last week. He had sores on his arms and legs. He was tired and lost. His eyes played tricks on him. Every once in awhile his father appeared from behind a tree and told him to read his Bible and to pray. He knew it was not really his father, but he talked to him anyway.

In the late afternoon from sheer exhaustion he fell asleep under some large plant leaves. He didn't hear the two boys who walked past him. His father appeared to him, and they talked for a few minutes. The boys turned around to check the voices they heard. There they discovered Paul Preston in a delirious conversation with no one. What they saw frightened them, and they ran for their father.

At first sight the North Viet Nam father knew the man was the one they were after. The boys needed some reward for finding him. Paul Preston was in no way fit to put up any resistance. The father gave his two sons branches with which to beat their new captive. The father encouraged the boys to beat the man until he was unconscious.

It was at this point Paul Preston found solace in a movie he had once seen.

Paul Preston had been raised in a Christian family. His father was a preacher, and the two of them argued most of Paul's four years in high school. Paul respected his father, but really wanted to get out from under his control. Paul's mother was killed in a tragic car wreck his freshman year. His older sister had been raped and brutally murdered his junior year. Losing his mother and sister put a severe strain on his relationship with his father. Getting involved with Junior ROTC helped him make it through those times.

As a young teenager, Paul saw the movie The Parent Trap with Hayley Mills. He really enjoyed the movie and fell in love with Hayley Mills. He heard her sing "Let's Get Together" over and over in his head. He could almost recite the movie by memory. That movie helped keep him alive and "sane" during his captivity. Often he'd withdraw from the outer world into the inner world of make believe in his mind.

After the boys beat him, the father and a friend drug him to a small village deeper in the jungles. There they dropped him down into a pit. Early in the morning his father appeared to him.

"Paul, Paul. Wake up, son. We need to talk."

Paul managed to open his eyes. He saw his father sitting on a rock beside him. There was concern in his eyes. He wanted to reach out and hug his son, but he just sat there like a frozen statue.

"I tried to tell you not to join the army."

"I know, daddy. I remember. But I didn't have a choice. I was going to be drafted."

"Don't you wish you had listened to me?"

"Yes, daddy. I wish I had listened to you."

"Paul, my son, you're in a fix now. What are you going to do?"

"Wait, daddy."

"Wait? Wait for what?"

"When the army realizes that I've been captured, they will send another team out to get me."

"You mean more of those green berets?"

"Yes, daddy. We're the best the army has."

In the distance Paul heard someone singing. It was a female voice, soft and sweet. The singing grew louder and louder. Then Paul recognized the song when he could make out some of the words. The voice sung:

> Oh! I really think you're swell.
> Uh huh! We really ring the bell.
> Oo, wee! And if you stick with me
> Nothing could be greater, say hey, alligator.

Paul sat up and leaned against the dirt wall. It was Hayley Mills. It was Hayley Mills. That statement sounded over and over in his mind. It was Hayley Mills. He pointed and whispered over to his father, "Look, daddy. It's Hayley Mills. It's really Hayley Mills."

Hayley Mills put her guitar down by Mr. Preston and knelt down beside Paul. She smiled at him. "I'm sorry you're here like this, Paul. I wish there were more I could do for you." Right away Paul picked up on her British accent.

"Just being here is enough, Miss Mills."

"My name is Hayley. That's what all my friends call me."

Paul was almost to the point of crying. Perhaps if he had more water to drink, he would have had tears to cry. "Miss Mills. I mean, Hayley. Am I your friend?"

"Why, Paul, you're my number one best friend."

"Do you mean that? Do you really mean that?"

"Yes, I certainly mean that."

The guards heard Paul Preston moving around and talking down in the pit. They went to get the man in charge. The guards told him the prisoner was awake and talking. He let them know it was time for more fun before they killed the prisoner. He told them to get the prisoner out of the pit and hang him by his hands from the tree by the pit. The man in charge called for all the females in the village. It was their turn to have some fun.

They pulled Paul Preston out of the pit. When they did, they dislocated his right shoulder and opened many of the sores on his arms and legs. He was so weak and pain-ridden that more pain did not matter. He had no strength to resist whatever they had in store for him.

The guards cut the rope and let him fall to the ground. As he lay there face up, the female population of that little village passed by, squatted, and urinated on him. By the time it was all over, he lay in a pool of urine. They left him there the rest of the night in the pool of urine.

About three o'clock in the morning Paul's father reappeared. Paul heard him speaking to him, but he was not able to speak back. His father was again reminding him of how stupid it was to have joined the army. He ought to be off at college studying and playing football. Paul wished his father would go away and his mother and sister would come visit him. He had forgotten they were both dead.

Paul passed out. His father left him. Again he heard the singing in the distance. He was sure it was his friend Hayley Mills coming to see him. She came from behind the tree. She was as pretty as ever she was in the movie. He was in love with her.

"Paul, I'm back to see you."

"But where is your sister?"

"What sister?"

"The one in the movie that looked just like you. Your twin."

"I don't have a twin sister." Hayley explained to Paul that it was just part of the story.

"That's too bad. The world needs two of you."

"But the real one is here with you now."

"I sure am glad. I need a real friend now."

"You do, Paul, and I will never leave you."

"Hayley, did you ever meet my mother and sister?"

"No, Paul, I never did."

"You should; they are wonderful people."

"I'm sure they are. Perhaps I will one day."

"Hayley, may I say something personal to you?"

"Yes, of course."

"You are so young and beautiful. I think you are the prettiest girl in the whole world."

"That is very kind of you."

"No lie. And I love your British accent."

Hayley Mills smiled.

"And I really, really like that song 'Let's Get Together'."

Finally, Paul passed into a fitful rage of sleep. He dreamed about his father, mother, and sister, and of course, Hayley Mills.

The next morning before Paul woke up; the guards poured cold water on him. They all stood around him and held their noses like he stunk. Paul's whole body was swollen. He needed food and water. One of the women threw him a piece of bread, and a small girl brought him a sip of water.

Then there was the sound of an approaching helicopter. The guards kicked Paul Preston and rolled him over into the pit. He fell the four feet to the soft dirt floor. Fortunately, he landed on his butt and was not injured further. The guards called for others and began to shoot at the helicopter. Paul Preston heard the helicopter when it was hit and exploded.

Some time later Paul heard the shouts and excitement above him. Then he heard another American screaming and asking for help. Then there was another shot and silence. The guards tossed the dead body of an American soldier down the pit on top of Paul Preston.

Paul screamed and stared at the soldier. The soldier did not move. His body was burnt beyond recognition. Paul was almost ready to give up hope. His body began to shake all over beyond control. Before he could scream out in total surrender, the soldier sat up and assured him that others were on the way to rescue him.

When the soldier fell back against the wall, Paul's father reappeared. "He didn't have to die, did he? What a waste? And you, my son, are wasting away here."

"Daddy, I joined the army and came to Viet Nam to get away from you. Even now in the middle of a damn war I can't get rid of you."

"No, son, I won't go away, and don't talk to me that way."

Paul looked at his father with much resentment.

Then came the singing:

> Let's get together, yeah, yeah, yeah.
> Two is twice as nice as one.
> Let's get together, right away.
> We'll be having all the fun.
> And you can always count on me.
> A gruesome twosome we will be.
> Together, yeah, yeah, yeah."

"Here comes Hayley," Paul said.

"Hayley, Hayley!! Is that all you think about?"

"Yes, sir."

Hayley Mills stood beside Paul. His father disappeared. "What's the problem between you and your father?"

"He's so righteous, so goody-goody."

"Did you ever think he meant well by his words and deeds?"

"I've tried to."

"What does that mean?"

"After we lost my sister and my mother, daddy and I grew closer for about six months. Then he got really bossy and protective."

"Perhaps the thought of losing you worried him."

"Perhaps."

"I bet now he really is worried."

"He's not going to lose me. The army will come get me. Wait and see."

"They need to come soon. I'm not sure how much longer you can last."

"I'll last as long as it takes. Besides, daddy is here, and you are here. That's what I need right now."

"Well, I do all I can to help you."

"Hayley, just being here. Just being here."

There was a commotion above outside the pit. The guards were running in all different directions. Then there was the explosion of a mortar shell and the screams of wounded North Vietnamese. The women were crying. The children were crying. Then another and another mortar shell explosion. Then the shots of M-16 rifles.

"Here's a pit, captain," shouted an American soldier.

"See if Preston is down there."

The soldier tossed the basket gate-top to the side and looked down. "He's here, and there is an American pilot, dead it looks like."

"Get them both out, and hurry. They'll counter attack any minute."

Three soldiers went down into the pit. First, they took up Paul Preston, and then the dead pilot. Paul Preston was still talking to Hayley Mills. The soldiers asked themselves what he was saying and who he thought he was talking to. They couldn't figure it out.

A helicopter waited on the edge of the jungle, the pilot and crew ready to take off as soon as they got Preston aboard. The Americans fought hand to hand for some twenty minutes before they were able to get out of the village. As they approached the helicopter, a lone North Vietnamese man shot Paul Preston in the back. He slumped as they quickly placed him in the helicopter.

One of the crew shot the man before helping get Preston settled inside. A medic started an IV and placed a bandage over the wound. As the helicopter lifted off, Preston lapsed into unconsciousness.

"How is he?" the captain asked.

"He's alive; barely. I don't see how he survived all this. He is wasted and bone dry."

"I told you they'd come, didn't I, daddy?"

"What did he say?"

"Something about daddy. Maybe he's hallucinating."

"Perhaps so. He has earned the right."

"You see, Hayley. They came back for us. We don't leave our guys behind."

"Yes, Paul. They sure did."

"Sing me that song, please."

Hayley Mills picked up her guitar and started singing "Let's Get Together."

"That's nice, but where is your sister?"

"She's waiting for us at the hospital."

"Good. I sure want to meet her. She's not as pretty as you are, Hayley, but she is a pretty girl."

"She'd like to hear you tell her that."

"I sure will. I sure will."

The helicopter encountered enemy fire twice before landing back at camp. At the first aid station, Paul Preston received more attention before being flown to the hospital. At the hospital a surgical team waited, ready to take care of him. The captain went all the way with Paul and waited until he was out of surgery.

During the surgery Paul Preston almost died, but the doctors managed to keep him alive. Deep under anesthesia almost at the point of death, his mother and sister appeared to him.

"Paul, you can't come with us yet. You need to stay and take care of your father."

"Yes, mother."

"Your sister and I are so proud of you."

"I'm glad, mother."

"We'll see you later. Bye, son. We love you."

"Good-bye. I'll miss you. I love both of you."

Paul's father reappeared as his mother and sister disappeared. "Was that your mother's voice I heard."

"Yes, it was."

"I wish I had been here. I wanted to see them. I miss them so much."

As the doctors were sewing Paul up, his blood pressure increased and his pulse sped up. The doctors were impressed but could not explain how it happened under those stressful circumstances. Paul knew why.

"Is that you, Hayley?"

"Yes, Paul, and I brought my sister to meet you."

"She really does look like you. It is hard to tell you apart."

"That's right. We're twin sisters."

Paul looked at the sister. "What's your name?"

"Heidi."

"That's a pretty name. Hayley and Heidi."

"Can we sing the song for you now?"

"Yes. I don't think the doctors would mind."

"It's time we got together."   Hayley and Heidi smiled and began singing.

Paul tapped his right foot to the rhythm.   One of the nurses pointed the motion out to the doctors.   They were amazed but pleased.   Paul smiled and sang the song with the sisters.   At one point his eyes opened and shut like a blink.   All the people in the operating room could understand were the words "let's get together."   However, they had no idea what they meant or with whom Paul was singing.   It didn't matter.   All that mattered was that whatever it was, it kept Paul Preston alive.

Later that day Paul woke up in the recovery room.   The chaplain was waiting, as also was the psychiatrist.   Paul spoke with both of them. He seemed to have handled the trauma of captivity and being wounded well.   The chaplain told Paul there was someone special out in the waiting room who wanted to see him.

The chaplain and the psychiatrist left.   Shortly, the captain came in. He had a letter and a medal.   He pinned the medal on Paul's pajamas. A lot of work and red tape were rushed through to get the medal that fast.   Paul had forgotten what happened before he was captured.   The captain happily filled him in.   Sergeant Preston was on a special one-man detail to discover and radio the whereabouts of enemy rockets that were preventing the American pilots from returning safely from their bombing raids.   Paul was able to locate both of the hiding places and to radio their whereabouts before he was discovered.   He spent almost two weeks keeping ahead of the enemy, using up his rations, water, and ammo.

The captain left and returned to his troops deep in the jungle.

That night Paul slept comfortably, but his father returned sometime around three AM.

"I got a medal, daddy."

"I saw. I guess you're a real hero. You have saved many men's lives."

"That's what the captain said."

"I'm proud of you, too, son. I've been hard on you, a lot of it uncalled for."

"That's okay, daddy. We both want mother and Alice back."

"Yes, we do. I've got to go, son. I'll see you later."

In his sleep Paul called out, "Hayley, are you there?"

"I'm here, Paul."

"I can barely see you. What's happening?"

"I've got to go."

"Go where?"

"There are other soldiers to help, Paul."

"I know. I bet some are worse off than me."

"This is a nasty war. A girl can only do so much."

"You did a lot for me. How can I ever repay you?"

"When you get back to the United States, tell all your friends to go see my movies. That would mean much to me."

"The song. I still can hear it over and over in my mind. It is the best song I ever heard. I hope when I get to be an old man I'm still listening to it."

Hayley Mills kissed Paul on the forehead and waved as she walked out of the hospital room. She knew he was a special person, and she would never forget him.

Three months later Paul was flown back to the United States. He was healing and almost his ole self again. He had some leave and decided to stop over in New York City. There above a theater were the words: Hayley Mills starring in <u>The Trouble with Angels</u>. He started to pay and go inside. Instead he put his wallet in his back pocket and continued walking down the street.

"Hey, man, you back from Viet Nam?" a teenager asked Paul.

"Yes, just got back."

"You need to see that movie. That British girl is something else."

"I know. I've already seen her."

Rolling Heads

The mishandling of a prominent but mysterious predicament trickling through our battalion jerked me from a life of relaxation to a tour in an asylum. I was the clerk in a medical battalion stationed in Iraq. It was our second time to be in the country. Because I trusted my superiors, I ended up in a private asylum for months. If it weren't for the hospital chaplain, I might still be there.

The predicament: The son of movie star Roger Benson, Paul Benson, was slightly hurt in a firefight outside Bagdad. The intent was to have him transferred back stateside, award him a purple heart, and discharge him for medical reasons. His father had lots of money and had lots of political pull. Unfortunately, Paul was released from the medevac station and returned to his unit. The next day he was killed in action. Heads had to roll. This is where my memory begins to get foggy.

Colonel Masters was our battalion commander. He was a surgeon. From the start good ole Dr. Masters gave Private Benson his personal attention. I never did figure out why.

"Put these papers in Private Benson's file right away," the colonel ordered me.

"Yes, sir," I replied.

Earlier that morning I saw the memo from General Shull telling the colonel to contact the captain and get the paper work on Benson's purple-heart started. I had already forwarded it to the captain. The memo also mentioned that Benson was to be sent back to the USA and released from the army. At the time I didn't question that because it came from the desk of the general. At that time I didn't know who Private Benson was and I had never heard of his father.

"Be sure and type up Benson's orders back stateside."

"Yes, sir." I wondered why the colonel yelled at me so that everybody in the ward heard what he said. It was a direct order, and he made damn sure it would be carried out.

I took the papers and files back to the office and began to work on them. About an hour and a half later, Dr. Masters came in holding two cups of coffee. At the time I thought it was funny; he never brought me coffee before.

"Here," he said, putting the cup on the desk in front of me. "It's been a long day. You need this."

"Why, thank you, sir. I could use a good cup of coffee. It has been an unusual day."

"Listen, Frank. When you finish here, I need you to go get some surgical tape from the supply room and take it to number three op room."

"Yes, sir, this will only take a few minutes, and I'll be on my way."

I started to feel light-headed and sick at my stomach. As soon as I stood up, I vomited all over my desk. I quickly grabbed the files and papers and wiped them off. I sat down in my chair. The office started to spin round and round. I guess I almost passed out. The colonel called for two medics.

"Take him to his quarters. He might be getting that virus our soldiers caught from some of the locals."

The medics helped me stand up.

"Sir, I need to finish here first and then go to supply for that tape. I'll be okay."

The colonel placed the coffee cup in my hands. "Here, take a few more sips. This hot coffee will help you feel better.'

"Thank you, sir. I really don't feel well."

"Go on, take him to his quarters and have one of the nurses check on him every couple of hours through the night."

I felt like I had a tourniquet on my brain and I had a surplus of delirium. I had this inborn desire to be submissive and even questioned my ancestry. The verdict eluded me. The war ceased to exist. For a short while I ceased to exist. I later learned that I stayed in my room for twenty-four hours and was then admitted to the general ward. When I came to, two MPs stood guard at my bedside.

"Where am I? What happened?" I asked. I was in a fog.

One of the MPs went for Dr. Masters.

"Frank, what came over you? Why did you do it?" The doctor had a nurse beside him. He made sure the nurse and the MPs heard our conversation.

I had been on the ward four days. I had no idea what was going on or what the colonel was talking about. "Do what, sir?"

"Private Benson is dead. You sent him back to duty instead of back home. He was killed in a firefight the next day. You signed my name to the paperwork. Why, Frank?"

"I don't know, sir. I don't remember any of that."

"What do you remember?"

"I remember getting sick in the office and waking up here with these MPs?"

"How long have you been using drugs and over drinking?"

"Never. I don't use them or drink."

"Frank, you don't seem to be telling the truth. Now, you're facing a court marshal. Tomorrow I want you evaluated by the psychiatrist."

"Sir, I need to talk with my dad."

"Why? What will he do?"

"A lot, sir. I'm requesting to talk with him, please."

"Frank, you caused a man to be killed who was to be sent back home with a purple heart and a medical discharge. That's what drugs and alcohol do to a person; they ruin his life."

"Sir, again, I ask to speak with my father."

The colonel threw a file on a nearby bedside table and marched out of the ward. "Let him talk to his damn ole man."

Outside in the corridor the colonel motioned for the charge nurse to come over. "Do you know who the clerk's ole man is?"

The nurse looked dismayed. "I'm not sure, Dr. Masters, but I think I overheard the other nurses discussing his next of kin last night. I think he is a senator from Mississippi."

The doctor's eyes widened and a smile ran across his face. "Senator Joseph Sullivan is on the Armed Forces committee. He is from Mississippi. He's one of the oldest men in the senate. He must have had Frank in his maturity. He is a power house by himself. Be sure that Frank gets to talk to him."

"Yes, sir. Right away."

The colonel went back to his office to ponder over the situation. I lay back on my pillow and asked over and over what was happening to me. Did I really mix up the paper work and send Private Benson back to duty? If I did, wouldn't I at least remember something about it? The last thing I remembered was getting sick in the office. Then I remembered the coffee Dr. Masters brought me. That was odd; he had never brought coffee before. He must have thought I looked tired or sick. I drank the coffee, and then I got sick. Was the coffee bad? I remember it tasted alright. Still, I wanted to talk with my dad. Then I realized what the colonel accused me of and how angry he seemed when he left.

A medic came over to my bed. "Your father is on the phone; you'll have to go to the nurses' station to talk with him."

"Thanks." I tied up my pajamas and trooped down to the station. I must have talked to dad about thirty minutes. I explained everything as I understood it.

"Listen, Frank, are you using drugs? I don't ever remember you being drunk."

"No, dad." I reassured him that I was clean of drugs and alcohol.

"Then what the hell is going on there?"

"I have no idea. I don't remember anything that the colonel has said."

"Okay, just stay calm, and I'll see what needs to be done."

"I'm supposed to see the psychiatrist tomorrow."

"Just be honest with him. I'll talk to you later."

"Sure, dad."

The next morning Colonel Masters came to check on me. We talked; rather he talked to me about fifteen minutes. He told me he would see to things in my best interest. At the time I trusted him; I had no reason not to trust him. Again, he addressed my so-called problem with drugs and alcohol. He would not listen to my side at all. He said I had time with the psychiatrist at eleven o'clock. The doctor was a good doctor and would help me. Then he left.

For the first time I really looked around the ward to see what was going on. Before I only shuffled papers and took care of supply orders. Now I saw how nasty and deadly the war really was. I heard soldiers screaming in pain. I witnessed dead soldiers leaving in body bags. I just wanted to go home and watch TV up in my bedroom. Why didn't I listen to daddy and go on to college.

Well, I didn't go to college; I joined the army. I ended up in Iraq, and now I was in a lot of trouble. Why? What was this all about? I didn't know, but the feeling in the bottom of my gut was not good.

When I got to the psychiatrist's office, the colonel was coming out. He nodded at me and kept on walking. The doctor invited me into his office. From the start he was hostile and most arrogant. Without ever letting me even sit down, he lit into me.

"Why don't you just admit you use drugs and abuse alcohol and save us all this time and effort? We'll send you back stateside and get you the help you need."

"What about the court marshal?"

"If we get you admitted for treatment, we may avoid the legal crap."

I wondered what kind of medical talk that was. I did NOT want to face a court marshal. I wondered what my father was getting done on his end. I told him I wanted to talk with my dad before I agreed to anything. That's the way things were when I returned to the ward.

Later that afternoon I talked again with my father. He sounded optimistic and explained to me his plans.

"Frank, I talked with the Secretary of the Army and with the Army Surgeon General. We all agreed to have you sent back home. I have already arranged to have you admitted to an asylum in Jackson. I trust the people there completely. That will give us plenty of time to get this whole mess figured out."

"Yes, sir. What do I need to do?"

"Nothing, absolutely nothing. Just let the army get you back home."

Three days later I was on a plane headed for the USA, a MP sitting beside me.

I wanted to advance my case and avoid dishonor, to duplicate my family's traditional and balanced life style, and to shout the expedient cry "I am innocent of all charges." I had time enough during the trip home to think. The MP had little to say and left me to all my thoughts.

We changed planes twice. My father met us at the airport in Jackson. He took us to the asylum outside the city. It was a large mansion in the middle of a jungle garden. It was peaceful and inviting. Finally, I started to settle down some. Dad assured me everything would be okay.

We went inside the mansion where my father introduced me to the director. The MP left after he militarily placed my records in the director's hand. He didn't say a word, turned and marched out the door. I had no clue how he got back to the airport. I really did not care.

I suppose the asylum was expensive. It looked like a castle from deep in Europe. Daily I expected to see a king or princess descend the stairs at any time. The staff wore this stiff black and white uniform. The director always wore his long white lab coat. The scenery was beautiful but stiff, peaceful but rigid. There was no room for freedom. Everybody was there for a purpose, and nobody was to forget that purpose. It clumped and floated in the air.

There were two real, open people at the asylum. We became friends after I got settled in and started my treatment. The two were my psychiatrist and the hospital chaplain. Both were as honest and receptive as a set of worried parents, especially the chaplain.

My first evening at the asylum the chaplain visited me. The rooms were not at all like the wards in the army. They were more like modern, upbeat hotel rooms, only without any phones. The chaplain was different; he didn't wear a uniform.

"Hello, Frank. I am the chaplain. May I call you Frank?"

"Sure, chaplain. Come on in. I've been expecting you."

I ushered the chaplain into the living room area and offered him a seat. He sat on the sofa and I in the recliner.

"I understand you are a clerk in an army MASH unit," he said.

"Yes, I was or I am." I felt comfortable and at ease talking with him.

"I was a chaplain in the army for eight years."

"Oh, really. Why did you get out?"

"I had a run in with a doctor."

"You might say I, too, had a run in with a doctor," I replied.

"Tell me about it," the chaplain urged me.

I settled back in the recliner and looked up at the ceiling, trying to recall the facts about my time in Bagdad. "My battalion commander is Colonel Leroy Masters. He accused me of drug abuse and getting drunk and sending a wounded soldier back to his unit where he was killed the next day."

"Did you say Leroy Masters, Doctor Leroy Masters the surgeon?" The chaplain sat up straight on the sofa and leaned forward. "Is he still in the army?"

"Sure. He's been in over twenty-five years. He talked a lot about retiring, but he said he didn't know what he would do with himself."

"I bet he wouldn't."

"You talk like you know him."

"I sure do. He was in the last year of his surgical residency when I started my hospital chaplaincy residency. I was in the ER the night he brought in a nurse student whom he claimed was hit by a car. She died that night in the ER. The police suspected something more than what he told them, but they could never prove anything. Leroy Masters was a person who always wanted his way. He was ruthless and arrogant."

"That sounds like Colonel Masters."

"Frank, something smells fishy about what happened to you. I need to think about this and to do some research."

"Good, I will tell my father what you told me. I'm sure he'll find all this interesting."

That night my dad and I sat in my room and tried to make heads or tails of what this was all about. My dad sat on the sofa where the chaplain had sat, and I was back in the good ole recliner. My dad looked older than normal. He looked tired, but he never looked out of control or worried.

"Dad, when are you going to retire?"

"Never," he laughed. "Do I look like I need to?"

"No, sir," I lied.

"I've got a private investigator looking into this Private Paul Benson. That has to be the connecting factor. I still wonder what in the past connects this Benson boy with this Dr. Masters. I've got a feeling that will help us solve this whole mess."

Dad left and I went back to reading. I always liked to read Ernest Hemingway's novels. At the time I was about half way through The Old Man and the Sea. I remembered that the writer had killed himself. Even in my situation I wondered what could be bad enough to cause a person to take his own life.

That took me back to thinking about my father. Once he had pneumonia. Another time a fellow senator accused him of lewdness. The senator just wanted to observe how charming and satisfying my father's reaction would be. Dad never fretted over the use of doctrine to smear him. He was not especially religious, but his moral standards were almost spotless. I gave up very early in life trying to be as good a man as he is.

A few days later dad had the information he needed. He called and said he wanted to talk with me and the chaplain. We were to meet that night in my room. I was anxious to hear what dad had to share with us. We met after supper. Dad wore a dark suit. He looked refreshed and younger. My new friend the chaplain wore a dark blue shirt and a white clerical collar. I wore the uniform of the day for the asylum: a pair of grey pajamas.

"There is a definite connection between the young private and the doctor," dad started.

"I thought as much," the chaplain added. "What's the connection?"

"Family. A son for a son," dad replied.

"I don't understand," I said.

"I'm not sure I do," the chaplain added.

"Let me explain," dad said.

Dad sat on the sofa. The chaplain sat in my recliner. I sat on the floor between them. I felt secure when dad was around. The chaplain added a sense of peace and certainty.

Dad continued, "Dr. Masters had a son. He ended up in Hollywood trying to become an actor but only became a second rate stunt man. He actually worked in two or three films with Roger Benson. In the last movie Benson talked him into faking a fall from the sixth floor of a building in London. There was a freak accident and the son fell to his death. I understand at the time the police investigation cleared everyone of the blame and simply called it an accident."

"I see where this is going," the chaplain interrupted.

"Me, too," I said.

"Well, you're probably right. The good doctor blamed Roger Benson and swore to get even with him, if it took the rest of his life."

"So, how did Paul Benson get over in Iraq and wind up in our MASH unit," I asked.

"Sheer luck," the chaplain answered.

We both looked at dad, expecting an answer.

"You're right. Paul Benson joined the army after failing in college, went into infantry, and got orders to Iraq. All that the colonel knew nothing about. He took advantage of the hand he was dealt and was able to get a son for a son."

"And I was the sucker who became the pawn in his hands?"

"That's right, Frank."

My father talked with the Secretary of the Army and the Army Surgeon General. That led to what appeared to be an army wide investigation. I was cleared of any wrong, and Colonel Masters went to Ft. Leavenworth, Kansas for the rest of his life. I never saw him again.

As I stated before, I spent several months in the asylum. Was I ever glad to get out! Roger Benson invited me to visit him out in Hollywood. He took personal care of me and took me everywhere. I met almost everybody in Hollywood. As I look back, it was one of the best times of my life. It is sad that Paul Benson had to die for me to get that opportunity.

The army sent me back to Iraq and to my old unit, a wiser man who does not trust those who are his superiors like he once did. However, I have a world of respect for hospital chaplains.

The High Cost of an Education

Luke was a crippled freshman involved with a worldwide sham that turned hopeless because the small print was legible. Like most other students Luke Greenley needed money to attend the state university. Coming from a poor family in California he had no idea how much a college education cost. Upon learning the amount he almost gave up any hope of ever attending college. That was until he met Abe Kennedy.

Luke grew up in Long Beach on the wrong side of the rail road tracks in the wrong part of the city. His daddy was a taxi cab driver who almost didn't get his driver's license because he couldn't read until he was thirty-five. His mother worked at a factory where the only shift they offered her was midnight to eight in the morning. Luke was an only child who grew up lonely and shy.

Abe grew up in San Francisco where his parents owned an apartment down town. His daddy was a banker who took to drinking while in college and was addicted to gambling from the time he started his banking career. His mother wrote a column for one of the city's newspapers which became syndicated some time while Abe was in junior high. Abe had two sisters and a brother. He grew up self-confident and conniving to get his ways.

"What happened to your legs?" Abe Kennedy asked, gaping at Luke Greenley's braces and crutches.

"A car ran over me in junior high. I've used these ever since," Luke replied.

They were sitting at a table in the student center. Other students walked back and forth in front and in back of them. Soft music played over the intercom system. The smell of hot dogs and hamburgers from the deli filled the large room. There was the noise of six guys playing cards at a nearby table.

"Is this your first day here?"

"Yes, and not a very happy one at that," Luke said.

Abe at this point really began to check out Luke Greenley. Was he the type fellow for which he was looking? Was he desperate enough? Could he sell? Luke's face showed the disappointments of the day. Abe noticed that Luke leaned over time and again to rub his legs. "Do you legs hurt?" Perhaps Abe could add Luke to his list of twenty other operatives.

"Yes, especially when I'm tired and a little depressed."

"I can understand why you're tired, but why are you depressed?"

"Do you know how much it cost to go to school here?"

"Yes, a lot."

"Well, I don't have a lot, and my folks don't have a lot. I could never get a scholarship and probably not even a loan."

That was exactly what Abe wanted to hear. "Perhaps I can help you."

"You? How?"

"Let's just say I'm part of a business that would like to hire you. You could help others and help yourself at the same time."

"Doing what?"

"Do you think you're the only one who needs money for college?"

"No, of course not."

Luke looked over at Abe with suspicious eyes. He wore nice cloths and shoes. The shirt even appeared to be brand new. It had been a long time since Luke got a new shirt. The biggest thing Luke saw was Abe had two great, normal legs and he walked without the aid of crutches. Abe was and had everything Luke needed and wanted. Why couldn't the two of them just switch stations in life?

"You want a hamburger or a hotdog?"

"No, I don't think so," Luke answered. "I'm not really hungry."

"I'm buying."

"In that case I want either one."

"How about both with French fries and a drink?"

The two new friends made their way to the deli. Luke ate like he was starving, and Abe paid. They discussed their families back home and their growing up years. The more Luke talked, the more Abe knew Luke was his man.

"Have you ever sold anything?"

"I sold magazine subscriptions in high school and had a paper route before my accident in junior high," Luke explained.

"That's perfect. Let me tell you what we do."

"Can we go outside? It's getting stuffy in here?"

Luke and Abe went out to the courtyard. There was a slight breeze. The smell of new flowers filled the air. One could hear the birds chirping. The sun was directly overhead. A squirrel scurried across the yard. Abe carried their two drinks. Luke followed on his crutches. Abe made it a point not to mention anymore the braces or the crutches. They sat in a swing with an overhead covering.

"It's nice here. I wish it didn't cost so much."

"That's not a real problem," Abe said.

"Now tell me about what you mentioned earlier."

"I can help you pay for your education and at the same time help you help others with the same money problem."

"How? I have no money. So, I am interested."

"Like I said before; my father is president of a bank. They have extra money at this time, and he wants to offer it at a special rate to college students. We have to make sure they need it; that's all."

"Where do I fit in all this?"

"Two things. First, you need money to go to college. Second, you have the skills to help us locate others in similar circumstances."

"I know others who need money for college. My father is not president of a bank. As a matter of fact he owes money to two banks now."

Luke leaned back in the swing. Abe slowly rocked the swing with his feet on the ground. Luke reflected for a few seconds on his childhood and his parents. They always worked hard and had little to show for it. His dad needed a new cab; sometimes his stalled when he had a customer in the backseat. His mom needed new clothes. It seems like she wore the same ones over and over.

"It takes a college education to get ahead in this world, as so many say these days."

"That's sure what my father has preached to me for years," Luke agreed.

"You father is a wise man."

"I think so. He doesn't; he gets embarrassed when he thinks about himself."

Abe stood up. "Let's meet again tomorrow and talk more. Think about what I said."

"I need money, and I know others who do, too."

"Where are you staying tonight?" Abe asked.

"In one of the old dorms in the basement. Where are you staying?"

"My father set me up in one of the hotels downtown."

That night Luke had a difficult time going to sleep. He thought about his father driving that old car that needed so much work. He could see his mother in the clothes she had worn for so long. He could hear the car as it braked before it hit him when he was still in junior high. He could smell dinner as his mother put it on the table as they often waited on his father to get home for the day.

His mother and father wanted so badly for him to go to college. They had planned and tried several times to save some money, but something always happened where they had to take it and use it elsewhere. Luke needed a break, and perhaps what Abe had to offer was just the chance. He sure hoped so. He was excited about getting back together the next day.

The next morning Luke met Abe at the student center. They went to some office building down town where Luke felt uncomfortable and out of place. Abe explained the company had an office in the building. The office was cold and over lit. There were all kinds of pictures of colleges in frames on the wall. There were also several pictures of people graduating.

"Nice place. Looks expensive," Luke said.

"It's not that bad. My father got it for a good price."

"Why did we come here?"

"This is where we work. This is our home. This is where you earn you college money and also help others pay for their education."

"Tell me how we're going to do that."

Abe sat down behind the desk in a black plush chair. He opened the center drawer and took out what looked like a contract. "Know what this is?"

"It looks like a contract?"

"That's right, and it is simple as all get out. Let me show and explain."

"Go ahead."

Abe turned the paper around to face Luke and started pointing to different sections as he went over the contract with Luke. "Just fill out this top part: name, address, phone, etc. This middle section explains how the thing works: they give us $300 to secure the loan from my father's bank. Then we pay the tuition, books, etc. and start them on a monthly $600 check to live on. The payback begins two years after they graduate."

Luke rubbed one of his legs and nodded his head up and down. "That sounds great. How much is the payback?"

"It depends on their job and income."

"When can I start?"

"You already did. Here are five contracts. Take them and bring me back the $300 for each."

Back at school Luke began to make a list of others who needed money for school. By afternoon he had twenty-one names on his list. Luke realized that Abe never told him how much he would make. He wondered how much of the $300 he would earn. Really, he had no idea. Whatever was more than he was making at the time. He felt his parents would be proud of him and his desire to get himself through college.

The next day Luke returned home. He had two weeks before classes started. He planned to use that time to contact as many other needy students as possible. He already had two in mind in his neighborhood. First, he wanted to explain to his parents what he had done to help himself and others.

The next morning at breakfast the three of them talked. The California sun was already high in the sky. The day was warm but breezy. The radio was on in the kitchen, and they could hear a man trying to convince them to buy a new car. Luke enjoyed the smell of eggs and sausage; this morning was no different.

"I met this other student at school."

"A friend already?" his mother asked.

"Not really friends like Jake and me. More like business associates."

"What does that mean?" his father asked, swallowing a mouthful of eggs.

"His name is Abe Kennedy. He is from San Francisco, and his father is a banker."

"That's a good friend to have." They all laughed.

"Well Mr. Kennedy has some money he wants to loan to poor students like me to help them get their education."

"That's nice. Many folk like us don't have a lot of money lying around."

"How do you fit into all this?"

"I help find students who need the loan and will take part."

"Are you going to take part?" his father asked.

"We never discussed that. All we discussed was my finding others and making money that way."

"Who are you going to talk to first?"

"I think I will call Mark Johnson this morning. He wants to go to college."

That afternoon Luke met Mark Johnson at his house. Both his parents were at work, and he was babysitting his eleven year old sister. She was watching a Disney movie. Mark and Luke sat in the kitchen eating Oreo cookies and drinking milk. They could hear the sister in the living room laughing with the movie.

The two became close friends after Mark was injured in a football game and walked with a limp afterwards. Mark suffered severe depression for about six months after the sports incident. He had had great plans for a football career. They were never to be.

Luke dipped a cookie into his glass of milk. "Does your leg still hurt as much?"

"The doctor says I'm getting arthritis in my right knee."

"That doesn't sound good."

"No, I might be on crutches in a couple of years."

Luke smiled and said, "That is not all bad; I've learned to live with it."

"I think you have done fantastic with your situation. I'm not you, however."

Luke could still see Mark running down the field with the football under his arm and half the other team chasing behind. They hardly ever caught him. For three years of his high school career he was the hero of all and the love of all the girls. Now Luke felt sorry for Mark because he simply took life a day at a time, without any ambition or any goals.

"How are the Dallas Cowboys doing?"

"Not too good. They need me in the backfield."

"Mark, you would have been the best football player of all time."

"Yea, well, now I'm the most pitiable of all time."

"Do you still want to go to college?"

"That's a crazy question; of course, I do. After this football injury, I'll never get into college. I can't afford it. I can't play football. That is hopeless."

"Oh, no, it isn't."

"What do you mean?"

Luke took a pamphlet and the contract out of his coat pocket. "Let me show you this."

"What is it?"

The sister let out a loud yell. An airplane flew over the house. A car honked in the street in front of the house. They both reached for more cookies. Mark stood up and limped to the refrigerator for more milk. When he sat back down across from Luke, Luke could see the tears in his eyes. It was hard to be a football jock and a cripple at the same time.

Luke wanted to help Mark; he felt sorry for him. Mark deserved to go to college. Luke tried to remember all that Abe Kennedy told him. He wanted to be truthful in explaining the program to Mark. What all did Abe say? How do I explain all this? Luke was much ill at ease.

"It is a way for you to go to college."

"Yea, right, tell me."

"It is a guaranteed loan. All you do is to pay $300 now and no more until you finish your college education."

"Then what does it cost me."

"That depends on your job and income."

"Luke, we are friends. Is this for real?"

"Yep, it sure is," Luke answered with pride.

"I need to show it to my parents and ask them for the $300."

"No problem. I'll call you tomorrow."

Luke left the contract and pamphlet with Mark. It felt good to help his friend find a way to go to college. He was glad he could help. He went back home. His mother was in the bed asleep, and his father was at work driving his taxi. Luke went to his bedroom to take a survey of what lie ahead for him after college. It was warm in the room; so he opened the window.

The telephone rang. It was Abe Kennedy. "How's it going?"

"Great. I talked to my first prospect today."

"Tell me about it."

"His name is Mark. We have been friends for a long time. He wanted to play football in college and then go pro."

"What happened?"

"He was hurt bad in a high school football game. He now walks with a limp. Football is out of his future for sure."

"Does he want to go to college?"

"He sure does."

"Did you tell him about our program?"

"I sure did."

"What did he say?"

"He took the pamphlet and the contract and said he would show them to his parents. He would have to ask them for the $300."

"You did what? He's going to show them to his parents? Why did you do that?"

"He doesn't have any money."

"Call him back and get that pamphlet and contract back."

"Why? I don't understand."

"It doesn't matter. Just get them back."

"I'm supposed to talk to him tomorrow."

"Okay. Just do as I said."

They hung up. Luke felt awfully uneasy about their conversation. Something was not at all right about it. He knew Mark would be out that afternoon. He decided to wait until that night to call him.

Luke picked up one of the contracts and read it. Most of it didn't make sense to him. I'm not a lawyer, he thought. However, he concluded it was okay and there was nothing for him to worry about. He replaced the contract on the bed table. His legs were hurting; he rubbed then a few minutes, took off the braces, and took a nap.

Early that evening Mark called Luke. When Luke answered he was in the kitchen. There was silence and then heavy breathing on the other end.

Suddenly, Mark blurted out, "You damn liar. You thief."

"What are you talking about?" Luke questioned, ignorantly.

"You know damn well what I'm talking about. I thought you were my friend. I thought you were really my friend."

"I am your friend. That's why I tried to help you."

"By stealing my $300?"

"Stealing? What are you talking about?"

Mark explained how he had shown the contract and pamphlet to his parents. They had no money, but they asked a lawyer acquaintance what he thought. Quickly the lawyer found the very small print at the bottom of the contract. It stated that another $300 was due before classes actually started. If the second payment was not made, the first payment would be forfeited, and the loan was voided. There it was: the whole thing was a scam—a quick way to get money.

Luke was caught totally off guard. He didn't believe what Mark told him. He denied that it was true or that it was even possible. He went on to explain how nice a guy Abe was and how his father was just trying to help needy students. Mark wanted no part of what Luke was doing. He preferred to believe his parents and their lawyer acquaintance. Mark's parents were totally put off by the idea, but decided not to cause Luke trouble if he would not bother Mark anymore. Luke agreed to that.

Luke hung up and sort of fell down into one of the table chairs. He didn't even notice the smell of supper cooking in the oven. He didn't hear the TV or the radio coming in from the other rooms.

Later that night Luke talked with his dad and mom about the whole affair. They didn't seem that surprised when they heard Luke share his story.

"Nothing is free in this world, son," his father warned Luke.

"I know that, but Abe seemed so real and caring. His father was a banker and all that."

"Having money is not what life is all about."

"Sharing and helping is a good start," Luke said.

"Yes," his mother agreed, "but the heart must be in the right place."

"It's not easy being crippled," Luke said.

His father added, "Crippled and poor is even worse."

They all laughed.

His dad got serious. "Tomorrow you need to call this Kennedy boy and get out of this racket before you end up in jail."

"Then you need to make sure Mark is okay," his mother said.

"When you go back to school, talk to the people in charge and see if you can't get into a work program of some kind. Then ask about all the loan programs and scholarships that are available. There has to be something suited for a young man in your situation."

"Luke," his mother said almost in tears, "I'm so sorry we don't have the money to send you to college. I wish we could and that it would not be a problem for you."

"I know that, Mother."

"When you have to earn something and it's not given to you, it usually means more to you," his father reassured him. "A college education is not free, and it's not easy."

To Love Is To Live

"Where did you meet this lady?"

"This is far out. I met her on the internet, on this program called StumbleUpon. I came across her blog by surfing through the system. She and I just started chatting."

"Have you met her yet, face to face?"

"No, but we have a date this Friday night."

My sister and I were sitting at a table at a sidewalk cafe in Rome, Italy. Pigeons were flying overhead and were walking around the customers who were throwing pane to them. One landed on our table, and my sister waved it away. She liked the pigeons but not that close. The bird landed a few feet away on the pavement, and my sister threw it a large piece of bread.

"Why are we having this conversation?" my sister asked.

"Because I want and need your advice," I replied.

"You want AND need my advice. You jest!"

My sister is two years older than I am. She has more education and has traveled more. She is married and has two children who are in college. I have never had a serious, successful relationship with the opposite sex. My sister is a psychologist who specializes in marriage and family. I am a writer who has spent most of my time in Italy after graduating from the University of Mississippi with a degree in journalism. My sister spent most of her life in college and training. She has always been on me about dating and having a positive relationship. Up to this point I never listened to her. I never wanted to.

"Yes, at this point in my life I want AND need your help!"

"How and why?" she seemed to get real serious.

"I got word from my publisher that they plan to go ahead with my new novel. That is three novels and two books on traveling in this great country. I have a very bright resume in writing. My resume on my personal life is not quite so bright. If this novel becomes a movie, too, I will have all the money I will ever need."

"That's good. Where do I come in?" Marshelle asked me.

"My dear sister, I am not really happy. Something is missing."

"You mean a home and a family?"

"Yes, I think so."

"You think so?"

"Alright, I'll go ahead and admit you have been right all along."

Marshelle smiled her victorious smile. I remembered it well from when we were children. She beat me at almost everything. She made better grades. She threw a baseball better and faster than I could. She swam better than me. She danced better. She made friends easier than I did. Her English was always proper. Where I was shy and had stage fright, she spoke with ease in public and enjoyed being the center of attention.

Writing was really the one and only thing I could do better than

Marshelle. In spite of my poor English I could put words together in a way that others liked to read them. I learned about my skill when I was in the sixth grade. I won an essay writing contest: a trip to Jackson, the capital of Mississippi. Later in junior high my writing helped 'put my name in lights.' I made good grades because of my writing. Three other students and I started a school newspaper that still exists today. In high school I took my first classes in writing and journalism. That is where and when my career as a writer really began.

After high school I attended the University of Mississippi and got a degree in journalism and in English Literature. I still love to read and to write. I also love to travel and therefore ended up living in Italy. Here is where I have done most of my serious writing. Almost everything I have written has been published. My work has appeared in some of the best newspapers in the whole world, on the internet, in books, and even in the movies. If you have heard of or have seen the movie "One Dull Day," I wrote the novel it was based on. That book and movie brought me a lot of money and the freedom to live how and where I desire.

"What is this girl's name?" Marshelle asked.

"She's not a girl. She is thirty-one and quite a lady."

"Okay, what's this lady's name?"

"Her name is Renee."

"Where is she from, and why is she here in Italy?"

"Renee is from Chicago and is studying art here."

"So, she is an artist, too."

"Actually, she is more into art history, especially Italian art."

"Oh, a scholar, not just one who is full of creativity." My sister prefers others who use the logical part of their brain, rather than the emotional/creative side.

"Yes, she's in the last year of her PhD program."

"Does she plan to teach?"

"No, she wants to live in Europe and work in museums."

A pigeon flew between us and Marshelle threw up her hands in surprise. Then she laughed at herself. She always looks pretty when she smiles. The waiter brought us more water and more bread. She plucked a large piece and threw it at the birds rushing around on the curb.

"I wonder if they will eat out of my hand?" she asked.

"Try and see."

Marshelle sprinkled some crumbs in her palm and held it down by her side. Several looked as if they were about to approach her but decided against it. Then one pigeon flew up and landed on her wrist and began pecking at the bread in her palm. Marshelle seemed relaxed. I thought I would get some good advice from her.

"Anyway, I need your help."

"How can I help you?"

"Friday night."

"So, you have a date Friday night. What of it?"

"Even at this point it doesn't seem like just any old date. It seems more special."

Marshelle turned professional. I felt like I needed to lie down on a couch to talk with her.

"In what way?"

"It's just a feeling, like when I get an idea to write something. It comes from deep down inside. It is a most pleasant sensation. It makes me feel complete and mature and hopeful." I knew that would give her something to analyze me about.

"In other words now you feel incomplete, childish, and hopeless?"

"No, not really. It's a longing, a yearning for something other than what one has right now at this moment."

She smiled and her face sparkled. "So, you are really looking forward to this date?"

"Yea." I shook my head. "I really, really am."

"Are you feeling paternal, domestic?"

"Now, I haven't thought of those particular words. Maybe so."

"Well, brother. In that case my only advice to you is to take it slow and keep control of those hot feelings of yours. Remember, this is not exactly like writing a new novel. In this case you are not the only one who determines the outcome."

I paid the bill. We walked down to the piazza and strolled around with the local Italians. Nobody was in a hurry. A man juggled balls on a chair at the corner. Another man played a guitar and had a hat on the street for people to toss in money. Marshelle pitched in a five dollar bill. I ask myself if he had rather have had Euros, but dollars he got.

That Friday night I took a cab to Villa Tiera and only had to wait five minutes for Renee. She was beautiful. She had long black hair like the Italians, but her eyes were deep blue. Her skin was clear with a few freckles here and there. She wore a green pant suit and a white blouse with ruffles in the front. She walked erect and proud.

We walked out to the waiting cab and I helped her get in. I got in beside her and told the driver to take us to a nice restaurant. I knew Renee liked to do things spontaneously.

"You look beautiful, like a work of Italian art," I said.

"Thank you. I have looked forward to dinner with you. Perhaps we can go to see a movie after dinner, if you don't mind."

"That'll be great, as long as I am with you."

"You are always so sweet and kind."

"Most of the characters in my novels probably wouldn't agree with you."

"I'm not just a character in one of your novels, am I?"

"No, of course not." I remembered what Marshelle said about this not being like a novel.

"I would hope not."

"No, you are a special lady, whom I have grown to care about." Slow down, I said to myself. Do not let those hot emotions get to you.

"Do you mean that?"

"Yes, I really do. I realize we haven't known each other very long but I already feel close."

The driver took us to a nice, small family café on the edge of Rome. I don't think I'll ever get tired of spaghetti and meatballs. That night I discovered that Renee and I enjoyed many common likes. She was absolutely delightful, full of life and love and language. Later we took a taxi to a downtown theater and watched 'Ladri di biciclette' (Bicycle Thieves). We both laughed until we were almost sick with joy.

It was almost midnight when I returned her to her villa. I told the driver to wait; I wanted to walk the lady to her door. He winked at me. Renee and I held hands as we strolled down the path leading to the door. You could smell the flowers in the garden. The moon was full and was in the middle of the night sky. The air was cool, and Renee shivered. I put my arm around her waist and pulled her close. She made no effort to resist. She gently placed her head on my shoulder. I don't know what kind of perfume she was wearing, but it grabbed me with a powerful force of love. Then, the warning words of my sister crept into my thoughts. Go away, I demanded. I do not need you at this moment.

Renee stopped outside the front porch and faced me. "I had a wonderful evening."

"I did, too," I said stupidly and childishly.

"When will I see you next?" she asked.

"As soon as possible," I blurted out without thinking.

"You know something?"

"What?"

"You mentioned earlier about how you felt in spite of not knowing me very long."

"Yes, and I meant it all."

"I think I know how you feel and what you meant."

"You do?" I tried not to sound too excited.

"I feel safe and sure when I'm with you. Like I will never die."

"You never will, if I have anything to do with it."

Renee smiled and said nothing. She resumed her position at my side and laid her head back on my shoulder. For the first time I heard the fountain at the side of the villa. We walked toward the fountain. Red, blue, and green lights flashed at and bounced off the falling water. A tiny black and white kitten meowed at the foot of the fountain.

Renee walked on ahead of me. She picked up the kitten and said, "How did you get away from your mother? You must be cold and lonely."

I heard the kitten purring from where I stood.

"This kitten has two brothers and a sister. I wonder where the mother cat is."

"Perhaps chasing a mouse or at the store ordering an ounce of cheese," I said.

"More likely at the store; she is a big, fat, lazy cat."

Renee held the kitten close and petted it tenderly. The kitten was quiet and content; neither of us realized that the momma cat was crying and hissing. Reluctantly Renee put the cat down on the ground, and it ran off toward its mother.

"I love kittens. It is so tragic that they all grow up to become cats."

"You are a special lady," I said. I moved toward her.

Renee moved toward me. "Thank you; I agree. And you know what: I think you are a special person, too."

We both smiled and embraced. I ran my fingers through her hair. She felt to me like she was purring. We kissed lustfully and fully. I have never kissed or been kissed like that before. I felt like I were a cloud passing over a serene pond. Then I rained, and the pond was more serene than before. It was like the cloud and the pond were becoming one. I did not want to stop kissing. I wanted that moment to last forever.

Two days later I met my sister for a visit at the hotel before she flew back to the United States. She threw all her training out the door and let her emotions take over. I wished I hadn't gone by to see her.

"You're going to do what? Are you out of your mind?"

"No, I am perfectly in my mind. I am going to ask Renee to marry me?"

"What about your future and your career?"

"She is my future and my career. I will be an even better writer."

Marshelle opened her suitcase and tossed things in it. "I need a drink."

"Fine, I'll take one, too. This is something to celebrate."

"How do you celebrate a disaster?"

"What makes you think it'll be a disaster?"

"Because I know you."

"Just what does that mean?" I asked.

"It means just what it says. You are no more ready to settle down and get married than a blind man is ready to walk a tight rope."

"Well, I'm not blind, and this is not a tight rope."

"One disaster is just as good as another."

We took the elevator down to the bar. It was about three hours before Marshelle's plane left. It was a beautiful day outside. There were some older children playing by the front door. There was a blind man begging across the street. I waited for Marshelle to compare me to that man, but she didn't. Maybe she didn't see him. Perhaps, she was tired and ready to go home.

"Do we want a booth or a table or should we sit at the bar?" I asked.

"Let's sit at the bar. It's more melodramatic like in the movies."

We ordered and we talked about the weather and the plane trip and many other things, but we did not mention Renee again. I was relieved. I love Marshelle, but she has always had that older sister syndrome. Out of habit I reverted back to my younger brother syndrome. I hoped she did not think because I didn't mention Renee again that meant she had conquered my feelings and my desires. She had not.

From the airport I took a taxi to the Fountain of Trevi. You may have already guessed that I like fountains. I threw a coin in the water when I first arrived. I envisioned the movie "Three Coins in a Fountain" and heard the music. I thought of other movies with scenes at the fountain. Here is where I wanted to propose to Renee. Whenever I traveled out of Italy, I always wanted to be sure I was able to return to my true hometown.

Now I wanted to be sure that I would always return to Rome with my true love. I threw two more coins into the water. Three factors of luck always beat one. I was planning my proposal. It had to be perfect. I just had to prove that Marshelle was wrong. I wished Renee was there with me then. Oh, well, I could dream and practice in my mind. Practice makes perfect.

Two lovers were sitting by the fountain; they spoke French. They were just teens. I hoped it was true love for them. Heartaches are not fun, and they spoil a lifetime. The girl was eating a sweet pickle and put the last bite in his mouth. He licked her finger and kissed her arm all the way up to her neck. Then they locked in a full kiss. I remembered our last kiss and yearned for more.

I took a taxi back to my room. I tried to finish an article I was writing for a magazine back in the states. My mind was not on the politics of Italy. It was not even on my novel. It was on Renee, and I could not break that thought. Finally, I stopped even trying. I was hopelessly in love. I took the phone and dialed down to the desk and asked them to call Renee's number for me.

She was not at the villa. I tried the museum where she studied, but she was not there, either. I really wanted to talk to her. I wanted to hear her voice and to touch her soft, warm skin. And I admit I wanted another of her kisses. For the moment all that had to wait. We had a date the next evening. I guessed I could do nothing but wait. So, I turned my thoughts to taking Renee to the Fountain of Trevi and proposing to her. In my heart of hearts I knew she was going to say yes; she just had to say yes.

The next evening I was a bundle of nerves as I prepared for our date.

Finally, the time came for me to pick up Renee. I took a taxi out to her villa. It was about six in the afternoon. I never tire of driving through Rome. There is never a dull moment. The Italians are so unpredictable. On the way out of Rome we passed a bad wreck. One man was lying on the road. There was a crowd around him. He looked dead or at least unconscious. One of the men in the crowd just picked up the man and threw him in the back seat of a nearby car. The taxi driver explained to me that the locals hardly ever wait for an ambulance; they rush victims to the hospital on their own accord.

We arrived at the villa. I looked back and saw the lights of Rome coming on. It was a lovely time for a date and for a proposal. Renee's housekeeper opened the door. She told me that Renee was almost ready and asked me to wait in the front room. There was a strange look on the face of the housekeeper.

"Is everything alright?" I asked.

"Our lady does not feel completely well," she replied in broken English.

"Is Renee sick?" I asked.

"I don't think so; she is only tired. She tries hard to finish her school work. It is important to her."

Then Renee entered the room. She was beautiful, but her face was flushed and she walked a little awkwardly. I stood up and walked over to her by the door.

"Are you okay?" I asked.

"Yes, I am just a little tired. That is all. I have been working hard on my research. I have this headache, an on and off fever, and my leg muscles ache."

"Would you rather not go out tonight? We can stay here, or we could just go out to eat and come back to the villa."

"No, no. I've been waiting for this night and being with you. I want us to keep our plans."

"Okay. Are you ready to go?"

We took a taxi to the Rivadestra Home Restaurant. It had the charm of "a living room furnished with care and elegance that makes one feel just like at home. Rivadestra Home Restaurant recently opened in the heart of Trastevere, the picturesque medieval area located on the west bank of the Tiber in Rome. It seats the maximum of forty-five guests. Its original front door from the XVIII century welcomes you into its softly lit atmosphere bringing back to memory Rome at its splendor. Guests dine around oak wood tables, surrounded by a relaxing and quiet atmosphere. Food selection varies every three weeks; a blend of new Mediterranean taste and classic flavors and aromas ably combined by chef Massimo (Max) Silvetti serving only fresh, seasonal ingredients. A fine, accurate wine selection includes more than forty labels: local wines are preferred. The Restaurant is closed at lunch time." So read the poster in the front foyer.

Right after we were seated and I had ordered us a drink, Renee rushed away to the ladies' room. She was gone a good twenty minutes, and I began to get worried. I asked one of the ladies at a nearby table if she would go check on her. The lady came back and said Renee would be out in a minute or two. I asked her if Renee was alright. She said she thought so.

When Renee came out of the bathroom, I knew right away something was terribly wrong. Renee was sweating and was white as snow. The whole happening made me feel sick.

"What's wrong?" I asked her.

"I am just sick at my stomach. I am so sorry, but I really think I need to go back to the villa. Do you mind?"

"No, of course not. I am sorry you are not well."

At the time Renee didn't share that she had been vomiting and had diarrhea and that there was blood in both. I took her back to her villa and left her in the care of the housekeeper. I wanted to take her to the hospital or call a doctor, but she would have none of that. When I left her, I assured her I would check on her in the morning.

On the way back to my room I worried about Renee and thought about the things I had planned to say at the Fountain of Trevi. Was it all to be trivia? Was it real at all? What would the morrow bring? Inside my coat pocket the engagement ring weighed heavily and sorrowfully. I could not deny that the feelings of love I had for Renee were real and permanent.

The next morning I called Renee from my room. The housekeeper was the one who answered the phone.

"Good morning. How is Renee?"

"She was hoping you would call."

"I promised her I would. How is she?"

Again in broken English, the housekeeper said, "She is much better and says she wants to see you tonight. She will meet you wherever you pick."

Here is my chance, I thought. "Please, tell her I will meet her at the Fountain of Trevi at seven o'clock."

"She will be there."

"Is she not at the villa now?"

"No, she had an appointment this morning that she could not afford to miss."

"I see. Be sure and tell her that I'll see her at seven at the Fountain of Trevi."

I supposed Renee was well since she was willing to meet me. I had no idea with whom she had an appointment; I guessed it was something to do with her studies or her work at the museum. I felt relieved and was able to return to my work. I spent two hours on the internet with research for the article I was writing. I completed my outline and the first paragraph. After lunch I went for a walk. If I lived to be as old as Methuselah, I would never grow tired of the streets in Rome. There is an eternal air of excitement and suspense.

Later I took a taxi to the Fountain of Trevi. I thought about that night and what I hoped was going to happen. I could see Renee and me as we walked up to the fountain. I could see us as we sat alone and the waters fell to the rhythm of our love. I could see us embracing and my proposing. I could hardly wait until seven o'clock.

Finally the afternoon passed, and six-fifteen came. I took a taxi over to the Fountain of Trevi. It was dark already, and the lights were on. If you have never seen Rome at night, you have never seen Rome. I wanted to get there before Renee to settle the nerves in my stomach and to make sure the proposal scene was as perfect as I could make it. It was perfecto, to be precise. I took time to watch the tourists as they gawked at the fountain. I suppose many dreamed of living in this great city, and here I was daily.

By seven-fifteen Renee had still not arrived. I stood up and counted as each taxi passed. There were twenty-five before one stopped at the fountain. A couple from Australia got out, not Renee. There were another fifteen taxis before Renee arrived. As she got out of the taxi, she looked like a modern princess presenting herself to her subjects. She was slender and wore a dark two-piece suit. I could not see the expression on her face. My heart leaped for joy.

I waved and shouted, "Here, over here."

She waved back and moved toward me. Then I noticed her steps were short and with effort. Her slender body was tilted forward a little. She carried a tissue in her left hand and wiped her mouth with it. I could not see the blood stains at the corners of her mouth from where I was.

"I'm here, finally. Sorry," she tried to shout.

"Sorry for what?" I asked.

"For being late."

Closer to the fountain under the lights I got a good view of her face and her mouth. She looked tired and worried. I took both her hands in mine and pulled her arms around me. She tried to pull away.

"No!" she said.

I pulled her back. "What's wrong, Renee?"

"I'm sick."

"You're just tired."

"No, I'm really sick."

"What do you mean?"

"I mean I'm in bad shape."

"Before you explain, I have something I want to share with you." I did not care what she had to share; I was going to propose to her.

"Come over here closer to the fountain."

With some hesitation she followed me. Fortunately, there were only a few people around the fountain. I took her over to one side, back into the shadows.

"Renee, I love you. I have never had the feelings I have when I am around you. I hurt inside and all over when we are apart. I want to spend the rest of my life with you."

"How about the rest of my life?" she said bitterly.

I ignored her comment and continued my proposal. "Renee, I do love you and I want to marry you. Will you marry me?"

"No!" she said bluntly.

"What? How? Why?" I stuttered and stumbled with my words.

"That's what I have been trying to explain, but you won't let me."

"Let's go to a quiet place where we can be alone and talk." I walked to the street and motioned for a taxi.

We drove around in the taxi before we agreed on Abruzzi. It was a restaurant near the Piazza Venezia. There were several students in the eating area. We ordered the cold antipasti only. The maitre'd offered us a booth off by itself. I think he could tell Renee was not doing well. The lights were dim, and there was a blue candle burning on the table. Renee blew the candle out, splattering a little wax on the candle holder.

"Excuse me," Renee said. "I need to go the bathroom."

"Sure. Be careful." I added softly.

When she came back to the table, she looked even whiter than she had before she left. There were blood spots on her handkerchief. I tried to keep my composure, but I was worried, really worried, about her.

"It time for us to talk," I encouraged her. "I asked you a question at the fountain, and you gave me a 'no' answer. I love you, Renee. Tell me what is going on, please."

"I am sick, very sick."

"I don't care; I still love you."

"I'm going to die."

"I do care; I don't want you to die, but I still love you."

She smiled half-heartedly over at me. "You don't need the burden of my condition."

"Let me be the judge of that; I want to marry you. Please tell me."

"But I cannot marry you."

"Do you love me?"

She took my hands and squeezed them tight. "Of course, I love you. My life has changed since we met. I am so thankful for that program on the internet. I felt like I was getting addicted to it, and it brought us together. Yes, I love you. It is because I love you." She took a deep breath and wheezed a little as she exhaled. "It's because I love you that I cannot marry you."

"I don't care what's wrong with you; I love you and want to marry you."

"I have a rare viral hemorrhagic disease for which there is no cure. I have two weeks to two months to live. I have not told my parents yet. I am scared and angry."

"How did you get such a disease?"

Before she could answer, it hit me hard what she had just shared. She was really going to die. And there was no stopping it. I could not take that. All I wanted to do was jump up and shout to the whole world "no, hell no."

"Remember I told you I went to Africa on a research trip? The doctor said that is where I got it."

"Renee, if you had two days to live I would still want to marry you. I love you, and that is all that matters to me."

"What I have is contagious through body contact, and there is no known cure yet."

"I'm not worried about that."

"You should be. You are young and have a wonderful career ahead of you. I don't want to interfere with that."

"You are a blessing to me, not interference. When are you going to talk to your family?"

"I thought I would call them tomorrow morning, after we talk tonight. I do not feel like flying home, and the doctor suggested that I not fly back."

"Do you want me to be with you when you call home?"

"No, I don't think so."

"Renee, I had it all planned out to propose to you at the Fountain of Trevi. I will try again here. Renee, I love you. Will you marry me?"

She started crying. A trickle of blood collected at her nostril. I wiped it off with my napkin. I looked at the blood. I looked at Renee. She looked at the blood and then at me. I leaned over toward her and kissed her on the nose and then on the mouth. She flinched and pulled away. Then she gave in and kissed me on the mouth.

"Yes. Yes, I will marry you, if that is really what you want."

"That is really what I want. We will face this thing together."

Renee and I were married a week later. Three weeks later she died. I took her body back to her hometown. I met her family. She had a brother who was three years younger. I easily fell in love with every member of Renee's family. We buried her body in the local cemetery. I bought a lovely bronze marker for her grave. We said our good-byes. I came back to Rome, just like I knew I would when I tossed the coins into the Fountain of Trevi. Each time I pass the fountain, I cry and think of Renee.

Marshelle flew to Rome after I returned. She was not able to attend either our wedding or Renee's funeral. When we met at the sidewalk café, both of us cried and embraced. At that moment my sister meant more to me than she ever did before. She held me as I cried like a baby.

"I am sorry," she said to me.

"Sorry for what?"

"Sorry for what I said when you honestly asked for my advice."

"I know you said what you truly believed was best for me at the time."

"I am still sorry, so sorry, for that and for what followed."

"While I am a successful writer, before I met Renee I had never really lived. Now that I had Renee, I have really lived. I had true love, and I lost that true love. But, my dear sister, now I have really lived."

Less than two months later I developed fevers and headaches, and I passed blood in my vomit and diarrhea. To me that meant I was going to be with Renee forever.

www.ingramcontent.com/pod-product-compliance
Lightning Source LLC
Chambersburg PA
CBHW030328030726
47499CB00003B/683